In the Shadows

Elle Klass

In the Shadows

Copyright©2022 by Elle Klass
Published by Books by Elle, Inc.
ISBN: 978-1-951017-30-9
All rights reserved
Editor Dawn Lewis
Cover art Getcovers.com

Author's Disclaimer

REALM WALKER

Books in the Realm Walker Series
In the Shadows
The Land of Lost Souls
Hidden Passages
The Ring of Betrayal

Other Realm Walker Companion Books
The Origin: Marya's Journal

Realm Walker World Books – coming soon!
Love at Frost Bite
Accidental Ghost: Soul Catcher Vol.1

Other Young Adults Series
The Bloodseeker
Zombie Girl
Hidden Journals
Baby Girl

REALM WALKER

1

A bundle of brown fur walked over Terra's face as she slept, tickling her nose. She popped a green-brown-blue eye open then pulled an arm out from beneath her and brought Clyde to her chest. He wriggled in protest. She didn't care. It was their morning routine.

The bedroom door moaned as it opened, followed by a deep inhale of breath. "What is that?" the voice of Terra's aunt asked in disgust. A rude reminder she wasn't at home in her comfy bed with the fluffy blue and black polka-dot comforter and snuggly matching pillows.

Worse, it was a reminder her father was really gone. She wasn't ready. At seventeen years old, she always pictured him with her at her graduation, her wedding, and all the other big moments in her life. The only family she had left was her ferret and she would move the Earth to protect him.

Buried in memories and her new reality, she was taken aback by the tone in her aunt's voice, Terra responded, "It's not a *that*. It's Clyde, a chocolate black-footed ferret." She thought to read her the riot act about how they were endangered but chose against it as she peered at her through a slit in one eye.

Her aunt's tiny mouth moved as the words caught up. "Where did you hide it yesterday?"

Deeply disturbed and enflamed by her aunt's tone, Terra sat up. "I didn't hide Clyde. He was in the carrier. The red one in the corner," she responded, pointing to the red fabric case sitting in the corner on a reading chair by the window.

Her aunt's face distorted in dismay and her tiny lips pinched together. "We'll talk about that after breakfast. Food is ready."

Terra let out a sigh as her aunt closed the door. She'd never heard of an aunt, much less ever met one. Who was this woman? Clyde jumped off the bed and slipped underneath. "She's a witch, Clyde. Don't let her bother you."

REALM WALKER

It hadn't even been two weeks since her father's death and she was sent to live with this woman who was clearly uptight and didn't like her. More than anything, she wished to be home with her best friend Noah. She picked up her phone, hoping for service but, like the night before, there was none. Terra dropped the phone onto the bed in frustration.

She hadn't known her mother, but from the stories her father told she was beautiful and full of life. She couldn't imagine how the bag that was her aunt was any relation to her mother.

She was a witch from her seventeenth century updo hairstyle that looked like brown bat wings to her pursed lips and uptight stance. Terra sighed as she pulled on shorts and a T-shirt. Not bothering to brush her straight hair.

Terra still couldn't believe her father was gone, stolen from her. He'd been the only parent she ever had. Tears dropped from her eyes as she thought about him, remembering his smile and the good times they had. It was a coast-to-coast camping trip in an RV when they found Clyde - or he found them. They stopped in Wyoming for a couple days. Clyde hung around their campsite then stowed away in the RV. They discovered him a few hours later. Her father laughed and said, 'I guess we have a new family member'. She dried her tears and smiled at the memory.

If losing her father wasn't enough, she was taken from her home. From their San Francisco, three-story row house on Telegraph Hill. The cars and noise of the city energized her during the day and put her to sleep at night. Now she was stuck in a small town that didn't have more than a few roads. The houses all the same colonial design, with thick pillar columns in the front and small covered patios in the back.

The start of her senior year she wouldn't be spending with her lifelong friends but in some small-town school. She'd only got in last night so hadn't explored much yet, but what she'd seen on the drive to her aunt's didn't settle well with her. A mixture of missing her father and culture shock crept into her guts and settled like a rock. All she wanted was to go back home.

The beige paint on the walls matched Terra's drab demeanor as she took a seat at the solid wood, octagonal table across from her aunt who took a sip of something steamy from a mug. A bowl of fruit and a plate of bran-ish muffins were set in the middle of the table. They resembled bran, but weren't quite the same golden brown as the ones her dad made. They were pale and looked sickly.

Light from the open window spread through the room but it didn't make Terra any cheerier; neither did the plants throughout the house, although they were the only source of color in the home. She grabbed a couple orange wedges and a dry bran muffin. Picking it apart with her hands, she played with her food more than she ate. The orange wedges felt more like apple slices, she dared not eat them.

"Did you sleep well?"

The woman obviously had no experience with teenagers, Terra thought as she responded, "I guess. I may do some exploring today." Her plan was to put Clyde in his harness and check out her new surroundings. Mostly, she wanted to get away from her aunt.

Aunt Rosette rested the mug on the table. "We need to discuss the animal."

There was no discussion. The "animal" as she called him was staying. He was all she had. "Clyde," she emphasized, "is not up for discussion."

Rosette pursed her lips harder as if to keep from blurting out what she really thought and cleared her throat. "You will have to wait until tomorrow to explore Provence City. We have an appointment at Provence Academy today. You'll be attending. It's a boarding school. You may come home on the weekends."

You may come home on the weekends, Terra repeated in her mind. *This woman has zero personality,* thought Terra as she painted on a snarky smile. "I just got here and you're already sending me away. Sounds fabulous! What time?"

Her aunt twisted her lips in a partial smile as if it was work to turn them upwards. "12:00 p.m."

Terra dropped the piece of muffin she was squishing between her fingers, stood, and marched back to her room. She didn't bother to push her chair in. Aunt Rosette. That's what she asked to be called but Terra thought of her more as Lady Betty the 18th century Irish executioner.

"I'll take you outside later on the patio," Terra promised Clyde as she glanced at him hanging off the wooden headboard. He was potty trained and used doggie pads, making his upkeep easy. As a ferret he was curious and liked to explore. He raced across the headboard and leapt to her suitcase before making his way under the bed and running up her legs.

She brought him into her arms and placed him on her shoulder. He liked to hang out there as she went about her life. He was coming with her to this boarding school. It angered her that Aunt Rosette was sending her away so soon, yet she thought it might be a blessing in disguise since she didn't like the pursed, uptight, eccentric woman anyways.

Terra's thoughts were interrupted by the light tap on her door. "Come in," she groaned.

Aunt Rosette, with her dark brown bat wings, stared at her with a softer expression than earlier. "I'm sorry. I'm not accustomed to having to care for someone else."

Terra glanced away from her and rubbed the top of Clyde's head. It was an apology of sorts.

"I'm not trying to send you away. Provence Academy is an excellent school that will teach you more than a school in the…' her voice faded as she recovered herself, "San Francisco. You really are lucky to get the opportunity."

What was that supposed to mean? There was nothing wrong with the school she attended in San Francisco. It was one of the best private schools in the area, but she accepted the half-hearted apology, guessing that was the best *Lady Betty* could do. "Sure." She wasn't going to say she was excited, as she wasn't. She'd expected to spend her senior year surrounded by friends.

Aunt Rosette moved closer, eying Terra's head. "We do need to do something with your hair and eyes today. Not much we can do about your skin."

In defense, Terra's eyes opened wide and she jumped up from her spot on the bed,

Clyde clinging to her shoulder. "What!" She didn't try to hide her dismay. Her hair and eyes were her best features and the ones she got from her mom. If this woman was really her mom's sister, she would know that.

She ignored Terra's outburst and handed her a wig the same bat wing color as her aunt's hair and a small plastic case.

"No way! There's nothing wrong with my eyes or hair!"

Aunt Rosette inhaled deeply and squared her shoulders. "Your father didn't tell you anything, did he?"

How dare she talk about her father as if he were inept? He was a highly intelligent, highly paid, computer genius. Terra grabbed the wig and case from her aunt. "I prefer you leave me. I'll wear the stupid stuff. Just go." Red clouded her vision. *What a heartless witch!*

She pulled the dark wig over her multi-colored, short-bobbed hair. Tucking the long strands on the left side behind her ear. In the case were blue contacts. The same blue as her aunt's eyes. They hid her natural hazel color. No doubt remained in her mind that her aunt was suffering from a mental illness. Appeasing her for the moment was easiest, as she wouldn't have to put up with her long since she was shipping her away to boarding school.

The walk to the school confirmed Provence City was no city and as small as she'd thought. There weren't even cars. A few people scooted around on hoverboards. The town had a strip mall called Provence Square, houses, and a circular building in the center named Provence Hall. That was about it.

In the daylight, she noted the odd teal hue to the sky and menagerie of flora that she didn't recognize. Not like she was any kind of botanist or nature-lover, but she recognized the normal trees and flowers. California, Oregon, and Washington were the only states to have Redwoods, so maybe it was the same here and they had plants that didn't grow anywhere else.

Memories of her trip to the horrid little town were fuzzy but she remembered flying in a private jet. It wasn't a luxury jet, but it was private. The flight took several hours, then the car ride took a few more. The windows of the car were tinted. The scenery beyond the window was barely visible – more like blurs. It wasn't until she arrived in Provence that she met her aunt.

A eucalyptus-myrrh scent carried through the air but there was no wind. With all the trees surrounding the city in a near perfect circle, it seemed odd. She was a San Franciscan and no stranger to wind. It wasn't exactly hot nor cold, but lukewarm. That would take getting used to. In California, they had excessive summer heat during the days and chilly nights, usually. San Francisco weather sometimes had a mind of its own and they'd have unseasonal wind, chills, or heat.

Aunt Rosette, who'd been quiet throughout the walk, opened her mouth. Her hair bobbed from the side as her cheeks moved up and down. "There are some things we should discuss before we get to the school. The residents of Provence are different than what you may be used to."

That was an understatement. The whole town was peculiar, but whatever. "Shoot."

Aunt Rosette turned her head briefly. Her eyebrows formed a V and deep wrinkles carved her forehead in confusion. "Excuse me?"

Terra chuckled. "It means go ahead and explain." She clicked her tongue and rolled her eyes in dismay.

"Oh… The students and residents of Provence are different. Each comes from a unique land and culture. They're not like others you've been around."

That was a mouthful of nothing. San Francisco was more of a melting pot than Provence. It's not like she lived in a small Podunk town in Alabama. "Ok, cool."

They followed the long road to a gate, but she didn't see a fence, just a bunch of trees. Her aunt pushed a button and the gates opened. A cement statue of a back-to-back wolf and dragon was the centerpiece of a water fountain in a lake. It was the only water she'd yet seen. The walkway spilling to a circular drive and a school that looked something like a V-shaped brick colonial hotel. Thick, double, wooden front doors were hidden behind brick arches that spanned most of the first floor.

The structure went up three stories at least, with matching cupolas on what she assumed was a fourth floor, and several visible chimneys. All the windows on the second floor and higher had bars over them. She gritted her teeth in disappointment. The place looked more like a jail than a school.

Terra let out a visible sigh and mumbled, "My prison for the next several months." Her aunt didn't glance her way and she assumed she'd missed her complaint.

2

The doors were as thick as Terra imagined them. Chills swept up her spine as her aunt opened the large door with a bronze pickaxe handle. She'd never felt more out of place and disturbed, yet curious at the same time.

Not a moan or groan came from the door as it opened. Not a soul was in sight either, giving her more chills that were soothed by the ornate interior of the school. The inside looked slightly more modern, like the houses. Sunlight teased the glass chandelier, spreading fractured rays of light across the lavender hue in the walls and catching sparkles embedded in the paint.

Realm Walker

Her aunt's heels tapped across the shiny wooden floor, echoing through the room. At the end of the entrance hall was a two-sided, rounded, floating staircase in wood that matched the floors. Large, ornate bronze pots built into the baluster contained cerulean flowers shaped like tear drops and deep green leaves that wove through the bronze gemstone-studded railing and banister.

Nervous and awkward, Terra stood behind her aunt; arms folded across her chest when she heard more clicking on the wooden floor. A woman appeared in a deep purple dress suit. Her blonde hair in a pixie cut, her smile warm and inviting as she introduced herself as Salena. She had natural beauty that went beyond the outside package, although her twinkling mauve eyes, taut skin, and slender curves made for a pleasing appearance.

Peace rested on Terra's head and wove its way through her person. She relaxed her stance without noticing she was no longer on the defense.

Salena walked past her aunt, parking herself in front of Terra. "Welcome to Provence Academy. I'm sorry to hear of the circumstances that brought you here, but we are happy to have you. I have paperwork for your aunt. One of our best and brightest students – Kinzo – will take you on a guided tour," she said in a sincere and musical voice.

In the Shadows

A hunk of eye-candy appeared to her right, his steps so light she hadn't heard him enter the room. His dark hair braided neatly in two rows on the sides and pulled back into a ponytail that trailed to his waist. His ears caught her eye as they were oddly shaped and pointy at the top, more so than hers. It didn't make him less sexy, but more so. That caught her eye first and then drifted to the rich blue of his eyes, similar to Aunt Rosette's color and the contacts she was forced to wear.

A tightish T-shirt hung over his broad shoulders, not leaving much of his toned chest and arms to the imagination. Cargo shorts hung from his waist and black canvas slip-ons covered his feet. *This school might not be so bad,* she thought as he introduced himself.

In that moment, it was only the two of them. Terra completely forgot about her aunt and Salena as she introduced herself during her eye-inspection. Heels clicking on the shiny wood floor brought her out of the moment and she wished she'd worn something sexier instead of the drab T-shirt and cut-offs she slipped on in protest at the ugly wig and contacts.

Kinzo folded his hands behind his back. "What do you want to see first? The stuff I have to show you, or the other stuff?"

Terra twisted her mouth. She really just wanted to take the wig off her head as it was starting to itch. "Whatever will keep me out of their sight."

He smiled. "We'll start at the top and work our way down."

Once they reached the top floor, she pulled the wig off. His eyes widened. "I like your hair, why were you hiding it?"

She fluffed it and shook her head. "My aunt made me. She's weird and, until I saw you, I didn't know anyone normal lived in this horrible town."

He tilted his head, taken with her hair. "It changes colors with the light. I've never seen that."

She chuckled. "Right! So why hide it? We should be proud of who we are."

"You're right about Provence; it's a weird place. Once you get to know everyone at the Academy, we aren't as firm and stuck in silly customs as our parents. Provence Academy is only fifteen years old. We'll be the first graduating class that started here the year it was finished. It's an all-grade level school," he said, his tone relaxed and friendly, yet she sensed he was holding back.

Old people were always the trouble-makers, stuck in their ways. They strolled the halls and she noted the door handles were shaped like infinity symbols. A few doors were open and she peeked in as they strolled past. They looked like dorms, large dorms. Two or three beds each, a walk-in closet, a couch, and plenty of floor space between the furniture, but the windows didn't appear to be the cupolas she'd noted outside. He explained that this wing was the senior dorms.

At least she'd have plenty of room. She crossed her fingers she'd end up with a decent roommate or roommates. "What's upstairs?" she asked, noting the staircase ended and she hadn't seen another.

He shrugged. "Nothing yet. I think its storage. They keep it locked," he noted, pointing to a door at the end of the hall.

Its infinity door handles and sleek wood beckoned her. She couldn't explain why, but she was dying to know what was up there. "Maybe not today," she lifted her eyes and met his gaze.

"You're trouble."

"Never." She didn't waste any time scampering to the door. The bronze infinity handle in her grasp, she pushed. Her hopes dashed when the door didn't budge. She thought maybe she'd get lucky.

He grinned. "Told you. Come on, I'll show you the classrooms and the main floor."

She'd find a way upstairs if it took her all year. The second floor housed the classrooms. Unlike her other school, there were no desks; tables of all shapes, chairs and even couches, but no desks. Boring. The two-sided staircase separated the high schoolers from the smaller children.

She slipped the wig over her head once they reached the bottom floor in case Aunt Rosette was lurking. The cafeteria was huge, with a variety of kiosks and an outdoor patio with tables. The books in the library were stacked to the ceiling. A few rolling ladders hung from the top shelves. She resisted the urge to climb up one and roll across the bookshelves.

For PE, there was a large sports arena inside. Seven unique flags hung from equal distances in the room.

The room she was most taken with was beneath the stairs. Shaped like a septagon, she noted the repeating theme. Each wall had an identical symbol to those on each of the seven flags and décor of the school. One contained a wolf head, another a dragon, a flask with decorative gold trim and a lavender liquid, an infinity symbol, a pickaxe, and a plant, in this case a tree, and a gemstone same as those on the flags.

"What are these symbols about?"

Kinzo's brows lowered in confusion. "You don't know?"

She shrugged, remembering her aunt's words from earlier suggesting her father hadn't told her about important things. She'd brushed it off at the time in anger. "What does it all mean?"

He pointed in the direction of the tree. "That's Serenity Tree. It's the symbol of my realm Aradia and located in the center." His arm moved to the dragon. "That represents Sier, home of the dragons. The flask represents Navarin and the wolf head represents Canida—"

Stunned and suddenly defensive, she cut him off. When her aunt warned her the residents of Provence were different it was more of an understatement than she knew. She reached toward Kinzo's pointed ear then brought her hand down. "When you say realms… You mean like countries?"

He studied her. "Where are you from?"

Their conversation interrupted by heels clicking against the floor and female voices.

She whispered, "Can you meet me later at Provence Square?" The strip mall was about all the town had and seemed the most logical place to meet.

He nodded. "Sunset."

3

Terra picked at the food on her plate. The patty had a meat-like texture and tasted something like chicken but different. The vegetables looked like mini squash, but tasted more like lemons. Hopefully, the school had better food. Her aunt wasn't much of a cook. At that moment in time her nerves were stuck between excitement and curiosity, not leaving any room for an appetite.

The scraping of Aunt Rosette's fork on the ceramic plate grated on her nerves. "I'm not really hungry. Clyde needs some exercise, so I'm going to take him around the block, but I'll clean the dishes when I get back." Adults usually indulged when there was a promise of taking work off their lap.

In the Shadows

Aunt Rosette eyed her curiously and folded her hands in her lap as if contemplating how to handle the situation. "The dishes will be waiting."

Terra fought the urge to punch her in the face. No 'have a good time' or 'be careful'. Nope, none of that, only acknowledgement of the chore she promised. Painting on a smile, she backed away from the table then rushed upstairs to the room, stuffing her aunt into the back of her mind. She strapped Clyde's harness around him. He climbed onto her shoulder as she slipped on a baseball cap and bounded down the stairs and into the fresh evening air.

The walkway surrounded in decorative grass layered with taller plants, their blooms sunshine yellow and pink on the ends. They hung downward, reminding her of Christmas ball ornaments. Their fragrance similar to cinnamon, but definitely not. Most of the house plants contained sweet fragrances giving the drab place some cheer.

The sky, having a teal hue during the day, danced with a rainbow of colors in the evening. She walked to the end of the block and darted across the street to Provence Square, otherwise deemed a strip mall. Its colonial structure and beams reminiscent of every other building in the town. Everything matched, like the town was designed and built all at the same time. It lacked character, unlike

San Francisco, which had a variety of newer and older construction.

Kinzo leaned against the brick wall at the far end of the mall. His dark hair styled the same and falling over his shoulders. She strolled past a few other people and gained a few gawks at Clyde. They acted like they'd never seen a ferret before.

Clyde crawled into her arms as she approached Kinzo who pushed off the wall. His lips curling into a smile.

"Who's this?" he asked, holding a finger under Clyde's chin and tickling.

The ferret only allowed people he liked to touch him which meant he approved of Kinzo. She'd done good and could trust him. "Clyde. He's a real black-footed chocolate ferret."

Kinzo's brows lowered in the same confused expression he'd given her in the septagonal room. "Where did you and Clyde live before Provence City?"

"San Francisco. It's nothing like this place. We had hills and people everywhere. At night, the lights of the city from Telegraph Hill were spectacular and Coit Tower is like a beacon that's always meant home to me," she explained, not hiding the longing in her voice.

They walked past the mall into the trees. "This isn't San Francisco, but we have something you might like," he said.

She followed him, caught up and kept pace with his long stride. "Tell me about your home. Aradia," she remembered that's what he'd called it.

"It's beautiful and green and colorful. The plants growing around the banister at school are eternal teardrops and native to Aradia. What you saw at the school, it's a part of all of us. It represents each realm. They built the school to teach acceptance of our differences. For future generations to continue the peace."

That didn't sound so bad and left one obvious question in her mind: "What is Provence City?"

"It was built as a place for five representatives from each realm to meet and find solutions that help everyone. Anyone can come here, but the only people who live here are the diplomats, their families, and others who work here."

Realms. That was still confusing to Terra. She didn't quite understand what he meant. She followed him into thin woods as they walked up a small hill. She hadn't even known it was there. Bluish, green, white, lavender, and silver leaves seemed to part as they approached, giving a new meaning to plants being alive.

"My mom was elected when I was a baby. She was part of the first tribunal and has been re-elected every five years for another term." He paused for a moment and turned to face Terra. "Anyone can go to the Academy. It's not limited to Tribunal members' children. Those of us with parents in town tend to go home for weekends occasionally, but those that travel stay the entire year except the midway and end of year holidays. For some it's too far to travel." He walked backwards a few steps before turning on his heel.

It wasn't her imagination. The trees moved for him. A silver leaf twisted sideways to avoid its leafy branches brushing against him. She walked towards it and paused, studying the curious plant, perplexed by its behavior. Clyde crawled down and sat by her foot.

From several steps away Kinzo called, "What are you doing?"

She glanced his way to see him staring at her with a silly smile on his face. "The tree moved. It twisted sideways because you weren't watching where you were going."

He laughed. "Of course it did. I'm elfin."

The words falling from his mouth foreign to her except in fairytale books and fantasy movies. There were no such things as elves. "And I'm a pixie."

Kinzo's laugh stopped and his lips twisted as if in thought. "Pixies live in San Francisco? Because I was thinking maybe you were a commoner with your colorful hair."

In the Shadows

She pressed her hands on her hips, Clyde running behind her. "I was being snarky. I'm human. Isn't everyone?"

His smile returned. "We're almost there." He turned again and jogged a few more feet to the top of the hill.

She joined Kinzo for a view of Provence City. It looked like an architect's plan for a neighborhood. All the houses spaced equal distances from each other. The streets in a backwards S. Two main roads connected like a backwards L. Provence Square off the leg. One street across from the square turned into the housing development and another road on the opposite end turned onto the back of the L. The back wasn't straight. It had a couple curves. The school was at the end of the back. In the distance were mountains.

All the homes in a similar style of construction, Rosette's house stood out as it was a medium blue with a small upstairs. Her room and a bath, that was it. From where she sat she saw her window, protruding over the downstairs roof. Inside the window was an alcove.

He sat cross legged on the grass. "Human?" he questioned as if never hearing that term before. "Hmm… That's why your aunt made you wear that wig."

She joined him on the grass, her legs stretched out before her, Clyde running over them. This was a lot for her to process. She noted his ears earlier and remembered her aunt's words about her dad and the residents of Provence being different. Words formed in her mind but struggled to leave her mouth. "Why aren't there humans?"

Of all the things she could ask. Why didn't she ask how there were elves, or if there were fairies? How did this place exist? The one question at the top of her mind was 'why not humans?'. Her aunt forced her to wear the contacts which she'd taken out as soon as they got home. She made her wear the wig that hid her hair. What was wrong with being human?

He ran the palm of his hand over the grass and didn't meet her gaze when he spoke. "Human isn't something we use. I think it means the same as commoner." His Adam's apple bobbed as he gulped. "Commoners are those that are exiled from other realms."

That set her off, not only did they strip the *human* title but tossed them all into a different realm. The only realm she knew. "We're criminals! People who have broken a law?"

He lifted his gaze to meet hers. "It doesn't mean you're bad or your family was. Part of this experiment is acceptance and peace. By bringing a commoner here we can learn to accept those from Lols too."

In the Shadows

Anger shot through her like a rocket. It wasn't Kinzo. He was kind. It was the stupidity of others. She was a token human who couldn't even be herself. Why did her aunt even bring her here? *Why not leave her in the human "prison" realm they called Lols? What the heck did it mean?*

Kinzo pulled his hand away from the grass and pointed towards the sky. She'd completely forgotten he'd brought her here to show her something. Her anger receded, left to fester in the back of her mind. Looking into the night the moon shone pink. She followed his finger as it moved, finding another moon on the end of it. A silver one.

"The pink one is over Drakonia, home of the vampires. The silver one is over my home Aradia."

Drakonia? Vampires? She was positive she'd never left planet Earth. He pushed his hair over his shoulder and his cheeks lifted in a grin. There were clearly two moons, as she glanced from one to the next inspecting them with a careful eye. They were identical except in color. They were twins, but that wasn't really possible. Moons were nothing more than space rocks and rocks were never identical; even splitting a rock yielded two different rocks. He was jesting. "No way! There's only one moon."

He turned, his sapphire eyes meeting hers, his full, kissable lips curling into a smile. "Which one is it?"

That was a trickier question. Physics wasn't her thing and she didn't know if the same laws applied here – wherever *here* was. She used what she understood. The moon collected light from the sun and reflected, but that didn't answer why one moon was pink unless it was reflecting on something pink. She took a guess, "The pink one is real."

"The silver. When in position over Aradia it reflects a twin over Drakonia. Blood River is wide, covering most of the area. Its red hue gives the "twin" moon a pink shade," he said in a tone reflecting how much he was enjoying teaching her about the realms.

Realms. Such a strange word. She'd always adjusted to changes, but this was culture shock in the extreme. *Was it even real?* If it wasn't, her mind had worked overtime creating him. "What about the other realms?"

"One moon until it reaches Navarin: a series of islands spread through the Lavender Seas. The "twin" moon reappears with a light lilac hue."

He brought a hand to her face and lifted her hat, revealing her long multi-colored bob. "Your hair gives away what you are and it's beautiful. The light from the moon gives it a silvery pink shade. You shouldn't have to hide who you are… but there are some who won't understand."

4

White hot anger raged through Terra as she flew down the steps, running into the empty kitchen then the living room where she spotted her aunt leaned over her patio garden. She had more than a bone to pick; she had an entire graveyard. Terra wasn't one to hold in emotions. What she'd learned from Kinzo festered all night as she'd tossed and turned. Aunt Rosette should have been the one, not Kinzo. She'd left her to fend for herself. Family didn't do that.

She slid the glass door open so hard it bounced when it hit the other side. "You need to tell me about my parents. Now!" she demanded, nostrils flared and eyes wide.

Aunt Rosette straightened immediately, glanced the neighborhood as a precaution. She didn't need nosy neighbors bringing this to the tribunal. Her own anger seething to the surface. The distance between them a few feet. She closed the distance quickly and pushed Terra inside then slid the door shut. "I've taken you into my home and that tone of yours has no place in this house or this land!"

"Fine. I'll get my stuff and be out of your hair. I didn't ask to be here anyways!" She turned on her heel to march upstairs. She meant it. If there was a way in, there was a way out, and she'd find it and make her way back home. A hand touched her shoulder. She spun around to see her aunt's face.

"You're right. There is a lot you need to know. We've only known each other for two days and much has happened in that time. My plan was to tell you everything today. Sit down with me and I'll explain." Her dark eyes softened and her posture wasn't defensive, neither were her words. They were almost apologetic.

Terra didn't disagree and was glad her aunt was beginning to see it her way. If Terra left now she'd never get the answers she wanted. She nodded and took a seat on the dark green sofa.

Aunt Rosette joined her, sitting on the other end of the sofa. The potted tree behind her twisted its leaves. Terra shifted her eyes to the other plants in the room. They didn't move, but she remembered how the branches bent for Kinzo yesterday.

"Your mother grew up in Meradin Woods in Aradia with my family. We weren't true sisters. My mom found her as an infant. She'd been abandoned. It's against the covenants to have intimate relations with another kind but your mom, like you, blended. In an elfin group she looked as much elfin as anyone. I can show you with my memories." She twisted her wrist and pressed on it.

A hologram filled the empty space in the middle of the room, playing like a silent movie. Two young girls running and laughing in a forest filled with green, blue, white, lavender, and silver leafed trees. Colorful flowers and bushes surrounded them. Terra identified her mother immediately. Her round cheeks the same as hers when she was a girl. She had the same rounded ears too. Watching her, she looked so alive, like she could reach out and hug her. A swell of emotions overcame Terra.

"Don't stop. I want to see more."

Sadness and joy filled her. Her dad spoke of her mom so much but never could he show her a movie. 'Your mother lives in you every day. There isn't another mother and daughter who are more alike.' Those were his words and through them she always felt like she knew her. The hologram displayed an older version of Terra's mother with a fiery-haired young man – Terra's father.

On her head was a tiara made from silver leaves and branches, an oval golden object in the center. The tiara her father had given her on their final Christmas together. She kept it in the silver box he'd given it to her in. It was one of her most precious possessions.

Through her memories and words, Aunt Rosette continued her story. Her parents fell in love and she got pregnant. It was forbidden and if a hybrid child was born of the union they'd pay the ultimate price: the life of the child. They were subject to the laws of their realms and the tribunal. Their only option was to leave.

Her heart cracked inside her chest, emotion flooding her. How could their union, or her existence, be wrong? What changed between then and now? "Why now, why me? Now that I'm grown, is my life worth more than an innocent baby?"

Aunt Rosette turned off the hologram and, as if for the first time, saw Terra as a lost, confused, and grieving teen. She slid closer and put a stiff arm around her in an attempt to comfort. "No. We've changed. Some of the covenants are harsh and anti-progressive. The old ways cause more harm than good. At the tribunal, we work together to find solutions that help everyone in each realm. We can no longer ignore the innocent ancestors of those we've exiled to the Land of Lost Souls. They shouldn't be punished for the sins of their parents."

Terra appreciated her aunt's sudden change from witch to something resembling human. "Where was my father from?"

"The highlands of Sier. The terrain is rough. Its residents fly mostly. Your father was a fire-dragon," she paused. "Instead of giving magic, Lols takes it, memories too."

Terra winced at the sentence. If it takes memories, why did she accuse her father of not telling her things and how did her father remember so much of her mother? That didn't add up, yet the memories she shared were vivid, convincing Terra that it had to be true. She also believed the tribunal was pushing for change. Kinzo confirmed the school was about acceptance.

The tribunal wanted Terra here and figured it would be easier to acclimatize the realms to a commoner if it wasn't shoved down their throats. She didn't agree. It was always better to be oneself, not a fake. She didn't want to cause trouble either, so agreed to dying her hair but refused the contacts. Rosette agreed, as not all elfin peoples had blue eyes.

With their bargaining complete, Terra agreed to pretend to be an elf. She wasn't sure that would work. It wasn't like she understood the first thing about them. Her aunt assured her the staff at Provence Academy knew the situation as well and it wasn't the elves that had a problem with commoners.

There was an edge to her aunt's words that she took as a warning. The charade was for her safety more than to give others time to acclimatize to a human. Probably why she was paired with Kinzo. She really despised the word 'commoner'. It was a way of saying they were less. Common, average, and with no magic.

After their conversation, Aunt Rosette fitted her with a clear, circular communication device like her own. The material cool and jellylike on the skin of her arm above the wrist. They didn't have or use cell phones here, which explained why she couldn't find a signal. It was a paperweight now, with all her memories stored in photos and videos of her father and friends.

"Thank you," Terra offered as she rose from the couch. Tomorrow was her first day at the academy and she still needed to dye her hair and pack. It wasn't like she'd unpacked yet, but wasn't planning on taking everything.

Her aunt stood and met her gaze. "Your parents' only crime was falling in love. They were never violent and left before they

were exiled so they could live a life together
with you. That's why you were chosen."

5

A more compassionate and less witch-y side of Rosette was emerging. Terra was glad she could drop the 'aunt' bit, at least at home. She understood she had to keep it up in public or at the school.

Clyde ran in circles around her legs then balled himself and rolled across the floor dangerously close to her backpack. He scurried inside it and peeked his head and front paws out of the top. She understood his language and he was saying 'let's get out of here'. Sometimes he preferred the backpack over the harness. "Me too."

She'd completed most of her packing and was ready to inhale fresh air. With so many plants in the house, it would seem they'd have an excess of oxygen and it felt stuffy. She carefully lifted her backpack and pushed her arms through the straps. Clyde rested his head on her shoulders.

She glanced at her phone on the dresser. It still had some uses even if calls, texts, and her favorite social media were out of the question. The cell phone stuffed in the back pocket of her shorts, she grabbed her ear buds. Listening to downloaded music wasn't out of the question.

When she rounded the corner of her street onto the next, she'd spotted Kinzo, or rather his side braids and long ponytail. He'd walked her to the corner the other night but she hadn't seen which home he lived in. He and a girl sat on the porch of a two-toned house. The entire downstairs, including the porch and its thick columns and half the upstairs, a tan color. The upstairs on the other side a gray. It was almost like the house was divided in half and squished together, the front door being the center.

She wasn't sure whose house it was — his or hers. The girl with him was dark-haired and wore a long plait down her back. They were perched on a porch swing. Neither saw her, their faces glued to each other by the mouth.

Admittedly, she was a tad disappointed, but hopefully Provence Academy had other non-taken eye candy. She wasn't the serious type anyways nor was she gender picky. Hot was hot! To avoid being a third wheel, she cut across the street and plugged her ear buds in, hoping they wouldn't notice her, being so locked onto each other.

Her phone contained several playlists. She was cool with all kinds of music too. Today she felt like dance music. Clyde's face tickled her neck as he wanted to listen too. She turned it up. The warning on her phone said not to listen too loud, but for her there was no such thing.

When she reached the end of the road, past the strip mall she cut across, remembering the foothills past the forest. The air in Provence City was wetter than California, but not nearly as windy or chilly as San Francisco, although, it depended on the day. Some days were miserably hot and all she could do was lie on the couch beneath the vent.

Not really paying attention to where she was going or how far she walked, music blaring in her ears, memories of home filling her thoughts and Clyde riding her shoulder, she stopped when she couldn't go any further. Her foot meeting an invisible shield. Pain shot through her big toe as if she'd walked into a glass door.

She dropped the ear buds. On the other side of the barrier were hills. It was absent of plants and appeared depressed, desolate, and bleak. Higher up was a waterfall she imagined dropped into a river blocked from her vision by the hills. The falling water was odd and matched the color of the late evening crimson sky.

"Terra!"

Someone calling her name caught her attention. She turned to see Kinzo alone. Where was the girl he was sucking face with? He jogged towards her. She waited for him to catch up. Maybe he had answers.

Clyde climbed over her shoulder and jumped. His little legs like spring loaded wheels, he caught up to Kinzo and walked with him. By the time Kinzo reached her he looked mildly winded like he'd run at least part of the way.

Unsure what to say, she sucked her top lip in then let it go. "I didn't want to interrupt."

"Nalysse is cool. You'll have to hang with us at school. There's a whole group. We could teach you everything about being elfin," he said, then touched her hair. The gentle brush of his hand sent tingles over her spine.

She rolled her eyes. "I hate it."

"It's cute. The first rule, though, is we wear our hair long. It's said to help improve our communication with plants."

Is that why the plants hadn't parted for her? She liked it short. Long hair irritated her. The whole thing made sense though.

Rosette's hair was long too, even though she pinned it up in the horrible bat wings. The plant this afternoon twisted as if to listen in to their conversation. Maybe there was something to it. The girl he was sucking face with had long hair too. "Is that true?"

"I don't know. I've never cut my hair."

"Really?" She walked behind him and pressed her hand above his waist where his hair stopped. "That's how long it is. If you put it down, where does it reach?"

He touched his leg beneath his cute, rounded ass. He then suddenly changed the direction of the conversation. "You found the curtain."

Terra was easily side-tracked and had nearly forgotten about it, although the ache in her toe hadn't vanished. Her mind refocusing on it, she forgot to ask more about reaching her magic which was what she planned on asking him next. For now, it took a back seat. "What is it?"

"It's the barrier between Provence City and the realms. There are seven entrances but the only one you can move through is the one which you are from," he said, matter of fact, like it was common sense and everyone knew it.

She eyed Clyde scampering and rolling in the dirt. He'd need a bath. "So I can only go through the human…" her voice lingered, remembering they had a different name for them, "… commoner door. I'm also elf and dragon and something undefined," she said, remembering Rosette had mentioned her own mother found Terra's mom as an abandoned baby. They knew she was a hybrid and part elf, but no more.

He rested a hand on his chin. "I don't know. There are no hybrids. It's illegal and breaks one of the most revered covenants by all realms. I guess it could be possible."

Terra turned, catching another glimpse behind the curtain. Her curiosity at an all-time high. It was right there. What a cruel trick for her to see it but not enter. She pressed her hand against it as a child would against a glass window watching the rain. The curtain dissolved and her hand went through.

Kinzo stepped back, his eyes wide and glazed as if mesmerized. "That's impossible," he mumbled.

She glanced at him as he stared into the other realm. "Can you see it?"

He nodded. "Even a hybrid can't be Drakonian or vampire. They are walking dead and aren't able to…" Clyde scurried between them before Kinzo finished the sentence. He reached down for the little animal but it slipped his grasp. "No!"

"Clyde," Terra screamed. Ready to save her little buddy, she lifted her leg to run and her hand was caught by Kinzo's before she stepped into the realm.

"No. Don't!"

She wriggled her hand free and crossed the plain in chase of the curious ferret who'd run up a hill and stopped. The rushing of rose-colored liquid from a series of waterfalls made it nearly impossible to hear anything else. Standing on his hind legs, his paws in the air, he froze. She caught up to him, collecting him in her arms. "I should have named you 'Mischievous'."

Glancing down, she saw what had captured his eye. A crimson red river. It wasn't a reflection of the sky or trick from the curtain. It was red! She was in Drakonia and that had to be Blood River. She hadn't taken Kinzo's words literally, that was her mistake, but if he couldn't enter the realm than he'd have never seen it.

Light flashed on the horizon, blinding her for a second. She blinked her eyes in response. When the spots disappeared, she noted what looked like tall buildings rising from the blood. The area was such a wasteland, maybe it was only a mirage. A metallic odor accosted her nose, forcing dry heaves. City or not, her curiosity took a back seat to her gut's distaste for the river.

Clyde tight in her arms, she turned around and moved off the rocks. A true blood river wasn't her thing. She couldn't get through the curtain quick enough to Kinzo, who waited on the other side. Another couple steps and she'd join him. A piercing wail silenced the whooshing of the falls, forcing her to cringe, followed by a splash. She stopped in her tracks, gulped, and met Kinzo's pleading and dread-filled gaze.

6

Kinzo couldn't waltz across the curtain like she did. There was no time to concern herself with that now, someone may be injured. To keep her buddy safe, she thrust Clyde into Kinzo's arms and stripped the backpack off her shoulders, tossing it at him. "Watch him," she ordered and scrambled back over the rocks, forgetting about the morbid river.

Instinctively, she fought the gagging and dry heaves to reach the person crawling from the river of blood. The splash from the blood fall made the tan rocks red and slippery as she stumbled down them. The person reached the bank by the time she got there and rested on their back. She felt a bit of relief as it meant they were alive.

"Are you OK?" she nearly shouted over the whooshing of the blood fall.

The person stared wide-eyed, all but their golden-brown eyes covered in red. "I think so," she said. Her face pinching into a grimace as she licked her lips. "Yuck!" She spat, scrambling to her feet. "Is that blood?"

Terra didn't want to answer that question. "We need to get you somewhere you can wash off."

The person, a female by the sound of her voice and round curves, became defensive. "Who are you? Where am I? We didn't pay for this!"

"Don't snap at me! I came to save your life when I heard you scream and fall into the river from that bl... fall." Terra caught her words, not wanting to add more horror to the young woman's day and pointed a finger upward.

The girl's face distorted in confusion, blood dripping from her cheeks. "This isn't a gag or something?"

"No. Tell me what happened. My friend," she pointed toward Kinzo, "and I will help you out." She crossed her fingers behind her back that Kinzo would help. He did say the elfin were more progressive than others, then she remembered Kinzo saying Drakonia was home to the vampires. Vampires drank blood. Did they prefer it fresh or from the river? Crap, she could be someone's meal gone wrong. "We need to move now, then you can tell us."

Terra's urge was to run over the rocks, but they were slippery with blood. Watching her footing, she stepped cautiously across the rocks. Her toe throb was a reminder of what happened when she wasn't careful.

"What kind of place is this? Are you sure this isn't a reality show?" the girl questioned as they made their way over the rocks.

Terra didn't have many answers for her. It was eerie to her too. "It's not a show." This was her new, unfortunate, life but it was looking better.

Once they reached the curtain, she breathed easier. The whole time messing in the realm she hadn't thought of the vampires occupying it and the dangers associated with that. Kinzo gawked at them in disbelief.

Terra put her hands out, palms up, elbows bent in front of her to say *what?*

His lips contorted, as if deep in thought with something to say, then he shook his head in dismay. "I know where there's a geyser. You can… you know," he said with a twirl of his finger.

They followed Kinzo to a freshwater geyser. Every few minutes, water erupted like a small fountain. Her name was Tania, she'd managed to tell them between gags and grumbling in disgust. She'd been spelunking with a group of friends when the cave sucked her down. It was her last memory before splashing into Blood River.

There was a lot to unpack, and she looked to Kinzo to do that, even though he seemed a bit confused and frazzled. It didn't surprise her he lacked any ideas and was more perplexed than she was. He hadn't gotten over how she was able to walk across the curtain when he couldn't.

"We have to help her," Terra said adamantly.

"A young woman drops from a bloody waterfall in Drakonia, where neither of us should be, and you think we have to help her. What if it was her time and you entering Drakonia had a ripple effect on the harvesters, or maybe it was a horrible mistake, but we have her and they can't fix it?" He rocked on his heels.

What was he talking about? She discovered Drakonia not the harvester home, and what the heck was a harvester? So many questions. When someone was in trouble, helping was the right thing to do. "Harvesters as in harvesting souls or bodies? She's very much alive."

"Yes, Thraves runs alongside Drakonia. When it's someone's time, their soul is harvested and their blood is drained into Blood River." The words fought to come out as if he didn't want to say it.

Eww! That was disgusting and more than she needed to know. Now that she was away from the dreadful death smell and had survived to tell about it, she jested at him, "You get queasy."

He jabbed back, "I thought you were going to puke your guts up."

They were both chuckling when a wet, but clean, Tania approached them. She looked like a shield maiden, with medium-length, dark hair shaved on one side and falling over her shoulder in waves on the other. Her skin a deep bronze with a blue studded silver ring in her nose and an armband tattoo on her upper right arm. The design was a snake eating its tail, or so it looked to Terra. Her golden-brown eyes studied them expectantly.

Rocked by her beauty, Terra lost her words. *Yeah, Kinzo was hot but Tania was smokin'.* It was Kinzo who broke the silence.

Tania listened, her face contorting various ways as she absorbed his words. Terra imagined she was as confused as she'd been, but didn't seem to harbor the anger Terra had. She'd also just lost her father. Her moods swung like a swing in a windstorm.

Tania's lips curled upwards. "This is too crazy for anyone to make up. I fell into a vampire river. That's so cool! It was gross, but who would imagine that vampires are real."

Not angry a bit. She was taking it very well. "We can help you get home," Terra suggested.

"Why the heck do I want to do that?! I'm a thrill seeker and this place is way better than home." Emphasized with the momentary widening of her eyes.

Kinzo had some answers, at least temporary ones. She couldn't very well go home with either of them, or be seen in Provence City, but there was a cave where she could spend the night.

On the walk home, Kinzo grilled her about the curtain. Her opening and walking across it seemed to perplex him the most. His mind couldn't get past it, nor was he able to see the other side. What he saw was what he called a 'spinning, teal vortex' until she stepped over it, then the vortex vanished. The rocks and river became visible. But he couldn't take one step on the other side. The realm curtain, an unseen barrier, prevented him.

"I guess you need to be invited," she chuckled at her joke. Kinzo wasn't amused, by the serious expression on his face. "You know vampires have to be invited in so… never mind." His eyebrows smashed further as she attempted to explain her silly joke, eventually deciding it wasn't worth it.

What he saw or why he couldn't step to the other side was the least of her concerns.

They had to help Tania get home and she clearly didn't want to, which made their job extra complicated.

"I have the magic touch," she quipped. "Plants are at your beck and call and for me the curtain dissolves and I can visit other realms. Maybe that's my magic."

"Impossible," he insisted.

They parted ways on the corner, not any closer to solving their little problem. The lights on in the house, Terra cringed as she opened the door, expecting *Lady Betty* Rosette to return. Instead, she was met with a forced hug.

"You took your comicay off. I didn't know where you were."

Comicay? Then she remembered the clear gel communication thing. "I took it off when I showered. I forgot to put it back on."

Rosette released her. "It's waterproof and indestructible."

That's what she thought. Terra had learned nothing was indestructible and if her father were there he'd laugh so hard his face would turn as red as his hair. She'd broken nearly every phone she'd ever owned. He tried the sturdiest covers and screen protectors. It was his mission to save at least one phone from an early death.

The one she had now was less than a month old and might actually last since it had limited use. "I'm sorry. I won't take it off anymore." Of course, she lied like any red-blooded teen. If that device could track her movements, she was glad she'd taken it off and, as a precaution, would take it off in the future.

Kinzo asked her to meet him at school tomorrow by the fountain. What had happened tonight needed to stay a secret between them.

Clyde, tuckered from the excitement, curled under the covers. He always slept by her feet then climbed up her body in the morning to give her wakeup kisses, as she called them.

Terra tossed her dirty clothes and reached into her drawer for PJs when a sharp pain like a stiletto carving into her chest erupted. She pushed her hand over her chest to lessen the agony and dropped to her knees. With each breath, her chest tightened.

7

The Tribunal

fledgling harvesters lost humans from time to time. Drakonia had a protocol of search teams and checking all entrances and exits through the curtain and veils to other realms. The ones lost in Lols, he guessed stayed as lost souls in Lols. There were pockets created by Cyrus that had never been closed. It's how the wolves found their way in and attacked them twenty years ago. Bane shuddered at the memory. Cyrus was dangerous and more powerful than any creature from any other realm. He had too much power to play with their lives and come and go as he pleased without a trace.

He digressed. They marked all the veils to other realms and kept them guarded, except Thraves and Provence City. Drakonia was a harsh land for a human and not survivable. The lowlands were covered in sandy rock worn by the Blood Falls – the veil between Thraves and Drakonia. Blood River wound through the realm like a corkscrew, carrying with it nourishment for a vampire. The cities were built on it. Tall, colorful buildings rose out of the river in clumps throughout the realm.

The search team found nothing, yet but the curtain had been broken. No comicay footage revealed the source. Bane wasn't ready to bring this to the tribunal. What happened in Drakonia was their business but… The 'but' lingered. Someone had breached the curtain. He would take it up with the Minister first. Nothing happened without her approval. She was the oldest vampire of the realm and ruled in their best interests not those of the tribunal.

They had a partnership with Thraves. His diplomatic skills were better served working with the harvesters who also had protocol for lost ones. Fledglings were young, and harvesting souls and blood was a task that took great skill. He admired that.

Few humans passed through the afterlife to become a vampire. The guidelines for one to earn life after death were stringent.

In the Shadows

As a human, he'd been a politician. A senator in Virginia before his life was taken two hundred years ago. He understood playing both sides and how to run a successful campaign. His work as a diplomat wasn't much different and the interests of his constituents and M'ra, the Minister's law, preceded all else.

Metford approached. A hand pulling his chestnut-colored goatee. Something the harvester did when he was nervous. Vampires and harvesters lived long lives, much longer than anyone from other realms. They'd had a friendship of sorts for many millennia and had cleaned up more messes than he cared to remember.

"Our search has come up empty," Metford stated. Colors swirling in his harvester eyes fixed on Bane. He pulled his hand away from the nervous tugging on his goatee.

Bane would never understand how the colors moved around the pupil in harvesters. It was dizzying to look at, which was why he never looked them in the eye long. Yet it gave them the special sight they needed to reap souls into the otherworld and communicate with spirits. "Comicays too?"

Metford nodded. "We see the incident as she fell through the cave but after that vision is lost. She vanished into Blood Falls. Our search and rescue team found nothing on our side of the falls. She has to be in Drakonia."

He was right. The falls dropped directly into his realm. A human couldn't fight their way up the falls and Drakonia, made of life after death, wasn't closed to humans. They didn't find their way on their own but through the veil between the realms. A human wouldn't survive any longer in Thraves than in Drakonia. The midlands; Thraves was a mountainous land. Fresh water from blood river ran through it, carving caves into the rock. The veil between Lols and Thraves thin.

Bane debated telling the harvester someone had breached the curtain. It might trigger memories of seventeen years ago and the cleansing. He was sure comicay footage would eventually reveal who it was. On the other hand, if he didn't tell him now, vampires might pay the price later. Of all the realms, they needed to stay good with Thraves. "Someone breached the curtain. Our comicay footage hasn't revealed anything yet, but we imagine it was nothing. Until we find out, we have guards set up on our side of it."

The harvester's eyelids twitched in response. "His location," he said, referring to Cyrus, "has never been revealed, but there are pockets in the otherworld where souls filled with deep loneliness and despair can hide for eternity. We'll send a team of our best into the otherworld to investigate."

In the Shadows

No doubt that was meant to appease M'ra and her witch hunt. "Until they return and we finish our search and review of comicay footage in Drakonia we say nothing to the tribunal. We get the word out to the vampires and harvesters in Provence City."

Metford agreed. It wasn't in their best interest yet to say anything to the tribunal and he didn't doubt the young woman would be found soon enough. The harvesters' description was a nineteen-year-old female, approximately 54kg and 1.7m tall, dark hair, brown eyes, and a nose ring. He'd bring this up at caucus with the other vampires today. The harvesters and most other realms preferred metrics but, as an American human before becoming a vampire, he still preferred standard measurements.

Bane and Metford went their separate ways, meeting up again as they strode the steps into Provence Hall with the diplomats from each realm. The building perfectly round, in the center was the meeting room. Seven flags hung from the wall at seven points, making a septagon. The seats in triangular fashion with the highest or longest serving diplomat for each realm front and center, the other four behind. Doors beneath the flags led to the soundproof caucus rooms.

Once every diplomat had taken their place, the secretary took roll and directed the agenda. The first topic: how the commoner in Rosette's care was adjusting.

The second longest serving elf on the tribunal, Rosette stood, her large hair casting a shadow on the wall behind her. "Terra O'Malley is adjusting. She was a little upset at first. Salena at the Academy suggested pairing her with Kinzo, who will be a positive elfin influence on her." His mother the longest serving elfin member of the tribunal. "He can teach her the ways of the elfin and Provence City. They've been spending plenty of time together." She wrung her sweaty palms behind her back. Terra wasn't malleable, nor was she what they thought.

If it came out what Terra was before the appropriate time it could mean banishment for Rosette to Lols and worse for Terra. There was no other option. The tribunal was set up to solve inter- and extra-realm problems but, more and more, each realm was closing in on itself and the veils were weakening. She feared the strife might ignite more war. Terra's kind was created for peace and maintained that peace for centuries. There wasn't a day she didn't feel the guilt of the cleansing weighing on her and all because of one of Terra's kind who forced an uprising.

The memories she'd shown Terra with the comicay were true, but the story didn't belong to Terra's mother. True, they grew up together in Aradia and were great friends.

Rosette's own mother found a hybrid elfin baby. That baby grew up with Rosette as her sister until she fell in love with a dragon. She escaped to Lols but she was never pregnant. There was no love child. Neither Terra nor the Tribunal knew.

Maglesh, the third longest serving troll on the tribunal, stood, his tail between his legs. "How is the comicay working on her?"

"Like it does on everyone else. No problems. We can access her memories, track her movements, and communicate. In Lols they have similar electronic devices they call cell phones. They are a bit more complicated, but she was able to acclimate to the comicay and her commoner device can't reach outside Provence City." Rosette continued to wring her hands behind her back. It came with nerves. Terra hadn't worn the comicay the other night and, even though she promised to wear it, the young commoner had rebellious and suspicious ways.

8

The dorm room wasn't difficult to find, it was her roommate that was difficult. She looked like a young Reese Witherspoon but had the personality of Rachel McAdams as Regina in Mean Girls. She was too "queen bee" for Terra, no matter how drop dead gorgeous she was.

Her blue eyes studied Terra's ears. "Do you have dwarf ear syndrome?"

She wanted to slap her into the hall and bar the door closed. Unlike full-blooded elves, her ears were rounded on the tips instead of pointy and they weren't as long. Pushing her rage down, she smiled. "Do you have MGS?" Short for 'Mean Girl Syndrome'.

In the Shadows

She huffed and turned to her dresser where she placed her neatly folded clothes into the drawers. Her name was Halsey and she was the Diama of Navarin. Terra, happy to leave that title as an unknown, was informed the Diama was the next in line to wear the crown and rule the realm of the fae. She was a land fae and could shift into a unicorn. On Earth, people like her were called entitled.

Terra laid a doggy pad on the floor at the foot of her bed. Halsey, who wasn't as busy as she appeared and as nosy as Terra assumed, made another snide remark.

"Are you a bed wetter or something?"

It took all her strength not to haul off and punch her pretty face, leaving a bruise that would shine like a star. She lifted Clyde's carrier onto the bed. "It's for him and he won't share the pad with you, instead he might use your bed."

Halsey's face contorted in horror and she leaped into the air, landing on her bed. Legs drawn into her chest with her hands. "What is that?!"

Terra sniggered as she unzipped the carrier. Clyde poked his head out, took one look at Halsey and scrambled under Terra's bed. "You scared him."

"Him? What about me?!"

Terra snatched him up and put him in her backpack. He didn't peel an eye off the scared, freaked out fae prodigy in a most awkward position. If the gel thing could read her memories, maybe she could use it for blackmail later? The thought amused her. "Don't worry, he goes everywhere with me like right now."

Terra dropped her gel comicay on the bed and flopped her blanket over the top. It wasn't going anywhere with her in the event it tracked her. Carefully, she slipped her arms through the loops of the backpack and exited, leaving her horrid roommate in a state of confusion. Tania gave her a reason to be excited. She had someone like herself – human.

Provence Academy was like any school. Students grouped together discussing their end of the year break. From what Terra could tell, they had two breaks during the school year. As a senior, by the time she was used to it she'd be graduated.

Clyde garnered many looks and a few comments over his mask-like facial fur. The fur surrounding his eyes was cream encircled by chocolate brown on his nose and cream around his mouth. His ears a similar pattern, chocolate brown inside and cream outside. No one asked or gave her quirky looks. She fit right in.

As promised, Kinzo was by the fountain and he was alone. He stood with his hands in his back pockets and didn't notice her until she approached.

He turned his dazzling sapphire eyes on her. "Did you meet your roommate?"

Terra rolled her eyes. "I just escaped her. Can we not talk about her?"

Halsey's reputation must have preceded her because he knew right away. "Halsey."

She nodded. Ready to change the subject about how unfortunate she was to be given the wicked witch of the school for a roommate, she asked, "Your girlfriend won't be mad will she? You know, all the time we're spending together." Not using her name was subtle, and meant as a spiteful jab. She didn't care. It wasn't like she was looking for awards on using tact.

"Nalysse will be here later," he responded, punctuating her name.

Trouble in paradise? "Well, we better hurry. We don't want to keep her waiting for her goodnight suckface."

He eyed her curiously, demonstrating he didn't entirely get her use of language but understood her tone. Choosing to ignore it he said, "Let's walk."

Once they were firmly out of everyone's earshot, including vamps and lycans who evidently had super hearing, they talked more freely.

"I still don't get it. You can't be vampire, and no one can walk into any realm."

She shrugged. "Maybe I can't walk into them all. That's something I need to figure out." She mulled over the strange pain that wracked her chest last night. Stress, she chalked it up to the trauma of moving to not only a different city but realm entirely.

"We might be able to find something in the library," Kinzo stated.

With floor to ceiling books, there should be something. "Yeah." She changed the subject because she didn't really care. It wasn't perplexing to her. "Why is the sky always teal here and there's no sun? Do you have sun in Aradia?"

He chuckled. "The vamps," like that was an obvious answer, and it was. "The daylight is bad for them. Not many things can kill an immortal, but direct sun is one of them. Provence is the place between all realms where residents from each can come. It has to be safe for everyone."

That made sense. She'd never considered it because she wasn't from here and hadn't known vamps existed until a couple days ago. It still blew her mind. "What do you see when you look at the curtain?"

"A reflection of the trees. You don't though, do you?"

She shook her head. "Nope. I see what's on the other side." Her mind pumping questions in rapid succession forced another to her unfiltered mouth. "All the plants are so colorful and healthy without sunlight, how do they survive and where is the water?"

He lifted his chin and tilted his head in thought for a minute before responding. "The light is filtered, but it's enough, and all the water is underground, except the geyser. It releases pressure. Blood River provides water for each realm but it's different. It goes through various filtrations as it travels through each realm. Trolls in Verboten are allergic to sea water, but mine jewels and metals and smith them. The water passes through in freshwater streams. It spills into Navarin which is covered by the Lavender Seas and by the time the water reaches Canida all the silver is gone as lycans are allergic to silver."

She didn't dare ask about the human realm. After seeing Blood River up close, she didn't want to know. "How about Tania? There must be somewhere on campus we can hide her."

"There's a movable structure the lycan crew stayed in while they were building Provence. I don't think it's used for anything anymore and I'm sure it's still there. Any more questions?"

She deserved that, but her mind changed course when she spotted the gel comicay on his arm. "You need to take that off." She pointed at the device.

Eyebrows drawn together, he asked, "Why?"

Elf parents couldn't be that different than human parents and the gel device had more to it than any cell phone. It was advanced technology. "It stores memories, calls people, allowing you to speak mind to mind. I'm sure it also tracks. Teen 101: Turn off GPS. In this case, the comicay goes. We don't need them finding us, or Tania, and we certainly don't need to share these memories unless you want to be kicked to Lols."

"Good point." He peeled it off and handed it to a tree branch. It stuffed it into a small hole in its trunk.

Good grief. She didn't even ask.

"Tania," she called, effervescing in excitement as they reached the cave. She'd waited all day to visit the fellow human stuck here with her and she was gone. They searched the cave and surrounding area but lucky for them she wasn't lost.

Kinzo's communication with the plants had a use. The trees pushed their leaves and branches in the direction of Tania. She hadn't traveled far and was lying flat on her back. "The sky is so enchanting."

Terra joined her on the blue-green grass. "I brought you some food. It's from my personal stash." She wasn't about to feed her anything from the school. For a snack, she'd tried something that looked like chocolate pudding but tasted more like someone's runny bowel movement. Her snacks wouldn't last forever. They'd have to sneak back to Lols and stock up, if only she knew how to get there.

Kinzo joined them, his palms resting behind him and legs straight in front. "You don't like the food here?"

Heck no! She decided not to be rude. "My taste buds aren't crazy about it. I'm dying for a juicy hamburger with several slices of Applewood smoked bacon, a pizza loaded with everything, or a huge burrito stuffed with beef and refried beans."

"Yes!" Tania licked her lips as she took the strip of jerky Terra offered.

Clyde jumped out of the pack and joined Kinzo, running in circles around him. "I've always thought ferrets were the neatest animals, but my parents wouldn't allow one in the house. They claim they stink." Tania rolled her eyes.

When the moon appeared, they all walked back to the campus. The mobile structure Kinzo mentioned was still present and empty. Surrounded by thick trees, she never would have found it without Kinzo. It looked similar to a school portable. A simple rectangular structure with a low V roof. The skirting matched the exterior with an easy flow to the eye. Lycans, or werewolves, were always portrayed as large in her realm and, evidenced by the four long bunk beds, that was true here.

To the right of the front door was a small kitchen, but it was open. Wood cabinets covered the wall broken up by a double sink and a refrigerator/freezer combo. In front of all that sat a wooden table and eight chairs. The bathroom wasn't much to look at either. The toilet was taller than what she was used to, but figured it served the lycans well and it had the other necessary requirements such as a sink, a small mirror above it, and a shower.

It wasn't built for style but function and lacked any décor except the forest green curtains. It was a drab place. However, it contained all the necessities and a fully functional bathroom. That was important for any human female, although Tania was a knockout.

Kinzo walked outside before Terra who whispered in Tania's ear, "I'll be back tomorrow."

Tania winked.

Kinzo held his palm out, a tree branch dropped his gel comicay in his hand. He pressed it on. The entire action was so smooth she wouldn't have noticed if she hadn't been watching him from the corner of her eye. She was elf, why couldn't she communicate with plants the way he did? The long hair thing didn't jive with her. There was zero logic to it. She opened her mouth to ask when two low voices waylaid her ears.

A few yards from their position stood a dark-haired woman in a yellow top and black pin skirt and a tall man in a suit. Terra spotted them from the corner of her eye and swung her arm in front of Kinzo to prevent him from moving forward. When adults met privately it was usually no good or an affair. In this case, maybe it had something to do with Tania.

Kinzo dropped his foot and glanced at Terra who held a finger over her mouth. "Two adults."

Branches dropped in front of them. They watched through the gaps in the lilac-colored leaves. Judging by the heat in the conversation, it was juicy. Terra strained her ears to overhear. She managed to make out 'a life lost in Drakonia' and 'fledgling and first soul'.

Was Tania the soul lost in Drakonia? The couple parted in opposite directions. Kinzo gulped loud enough Terra heard his nerves.

"That was a harvester and a vampire."

She rocked on her feet and whispered, "Tania?"

He nodded, giving her an *I told you so* look, but didn't say anything. He didn't have to. His facial expressions and body language said the rest. Neither of them could utter a word.

Halsey was out when she returned to the dorm. She hated to leave Clyde alone too long if the fae-wench returned. Turning the shower nozzle off, she grabbed a fluffy towel and wrapped it around herself as she stepped out, her mind mulling over the conversation and how much trouble they might be in if anyone found out about Tania and her little trip to Drakonia. She doubted her charm would be enough and was sure they'd broken at least one covenant.

She pulled on her favorite sleeper boxers then dropped the towel to replace it with a long, worn T. That's when she noticed a black mark on her chest at the eight o'clock position. On closer inspection, it was an infinity symbol like the door handles of the school.

She winced, remembering the pain like a stiletto carving into her. It hurt worse than the tattoo she got on her ankle. It was her dad who took her. The memory flooded her. She glanced down at the pink carnation tattoo in remembrance of her mother's undying love. Touching it gave her a sense that her mother was still with her.

9

Terra lay with arms folded on the grass behind the portable next to Tania. The sky gave the appearance of the sun rising and it grew lighter. At night, it gave the illusion of a sunset with brilliant shades or reds, pinks, and gold spreading across the horizon but it was absent of a sun. Darkness followed, lit with the moon and stars that reminded her of the glow-in-the-dark stickers one could buy from any variety store and place on the ceiling. Was the moon Kinzo claimed was real, true?

Provence City was climate and light controlled. It was like living in a snow globe. The curtain was the glass that trapped them inside. The trees shed the scent of eucalyptus and myrrh.

She'd woken up early, excited to see Tania. It wasn't only her humanity, but her. She felt something beyond kinship sparking between them; at least she felt it went both ways. Her dried fruit and jerky wouldn't feed them both for long and it might be safer for Tania to return permanently. That was the plan, but a part of Terra wanted her to stay and Tania seemed taken with Provence. It wasn't smart. They'd all be in trouble.

After overhearing the discussion between the vampire and harvester, a sense of urgency and dread forced her to toss and turn all night. Returning Terra to Lols was a pressing matter. She needed her to understand that. "Yesterday, when Kinzo and I were almost to the Academy, we overheard something. I understand very little about these realms, but their conversation was about you. They know you're somewhere and will be looking for you." She was so glad she'd forgotten her comicay the day she entered Drakonia.

Tania rolled her head to the side to take in Terra's profile. "I can take care of myself. I have survival and fighting skills. I'll be fine."

Terra rolled her head towards Tania. Their faces close enough she felt her warm breath on her cheek. "You have to understand these creatures aren't human. Elves communicate with plants, vampires and lycans have super hearing, vision, and probably strength. The size of those beds shows you how large lycans are. You may not be a match for them. Be careful, OK?"

"I will," Tania promised.

Terra hoped her promise was sincere. Before she left, she had one more thing. She couldn't show this to anyone but her. Sitting up, she pulled her shirt down, revealing the infinity symbol on her chest. It wasn't larger than a nickel but it appeared after she found Terra, after she entered Drakonia. It was the vampire symbol she remembered from the school. Every door handle being the symbol, it was difficult to forget.

Tania ran her finger over it. Emotions that she'd never felt swept over Terra with Tania's gentle touch on her breast.

"Wow! That's so cool and creepy. I don't have any marks and we're both human. I was there too. What do you think it means?"

Terra shrugged. "I don't know, but let's keep it secret." In this strange new world, she felt others knowing less gave her an edge. Each day she trusted it less and felt a growing need to explore the other realms.

Clyde settled on Tania's lap, showing he trusted her. "He can stay," Tania suggested. "It would be nice to have some company."

REALM WALKER

Clyde was very able to take care of himself, and she'd always trusted his impeccable instincts, even when they brought her into a new realm. If she hadn't chased him into Drakonia she wouldn't have found Tania. Instead, Tania's soul would be harvested and her blood part of Blood River. Leaving him also gave her a reason to come back; not that she felt she needed one.

Classes were different than in human school. Math didn't change in any realm. She breathed a sigh of relief she didn't have to take another math class. It wasn't her best subject. She sighed when she saw Elfin Alchemy L2. She'd already taken biology, chemistry, and physics. The latter was above her head and she was lucky to manage a low C. The other classes on her schedule were Elfin History, Diplomatic Relations and the Realms, Plant Connections, and Finding and Controlling Magic.

The good thing. Out of the five classes she had three days a week free since all classes worked on block scheduling and were only provided once a week.

Her first class, Elfin History, was OK. Like all history classes, it dragged on, but was interesting since it was all new to her unlike learning World or US history again, something she felt was taught too many times in human schools. The history of elves was something different.

In the Shadows

She glanced at the kiosk menus, her taste buds coiling in disgust, but chose something that looked close to a veggie wrap and water. Carrying her tray, she found Kinzo and his group right where he'd said in the courtyard outside the cafeteria. Winding through the other students mingling and working towards their groups it took her a moment to reach them.

They weren't only elves. Her knowledge limited, she wasn't sure what the rest of them were. Kinzo's girlfriend was perched next to him, dressed in a cute lace silky top and short, matching skirt. She looked the perky cheerleader type, but imagined all that hair of hers would make sports uncomfortable at the least and out of the question. She was stunning with her bright green eyes and long, dark hair. It wasn't plaited today but fell over her shoulders in waves that reached beneath the height of the table. She couldn't help but be curious about her eye color. Up till this moment, she thought all elves had eyes in shades of blue.

The twinge of jealousy she felt the day she walked past them was absent since meeting Tania. She'd captured something in Terra that she couldn't quite explain.

Next to his girlfriend sat a darker-skinned young woman with the most fantastic deep-brown eyes. Her long, dark hair in what she'd always heard called Senegalese twists. She introduced herself as Meesha.

Next to her, a male elf, who introduced himself as Caspen, his hair curly-wild like a head-jungle. It didn't look long, but she imagined if she pulled a lock it would extend down his back. Next to him, a female vampire – Hyacinth. Her hair black and straight as a board, and she wore the cutest outfit; a pin skirt, tight blouse that hugged her small curves, and platform shoes. As a human, all Terra knew of vampires was what was portrayed in the movies. Vampires were usually gorgeous, but Hyacinth looked quite human if not a tad pale. She wasn't any more stunning than anyone else. The chemistry between Caspen and Hyacinth was impossible not to notice. She giggled inside. Obviously, the young weren't so stuck in the old ways.

Last in the group was a fairy – Kayln. She was on the rounder side, but her lavender hair and chiseled features gave it away as well as her pride. The sense of entitlement seemed to run in the fae. Terra liked her style, as she dressed in a cute, pleated skirt and lace knee stockings. She didn't waste a second announcing she was a water fae who was born in the Lavender Seas.

Her announcement was followed by an eye roll from Meesha. "Ignore her. We do. How are things going?"

There wasn't much to say yet, so she brought up her schedule and instructors. When she mentioned Finding and Controlling Magic with instructor Gwond everyone glanced to each other in a secret language that she understood. This wasn't a class she wanted.

It was Meesha who spoke again. "That class is young students. You don't want to be the only one more than ten years old. I think I have a solution. I'm Gwond's best student. He teaches advanced level classes and I think we can talk to him and he'll agree to let me be your tutor during class time." She paused. "If you're good with a lycan instructor."

She was a lycan, and a very striking one as well as friendly. She already liked her. "Yeah, that would be great. Are you sure?"

"You mean because you're elfin, or because it would take time out of my schedule?"

Terra shrugged. "Both, I guess. Don't want to be a burden."

Caspen spoke, "Meesha's the best at reaching and controlling magic. All magic is really the same, it just affects us all different. Whatever yours is, she'll help you find it."

His confidence made Terra surer she wanted the lycan teaching her.

Kayln bubbled in her seat as if about to pop her cork. "Is it true?" she asked very quietly, her question aimed at Terra.

"What?" Terra asked, unsure what she was talking about. All their eyes shifted and met once more in the silent language, only this time she didn't understand.

"That you're, you know, a commoner," Kayln's voice barely a whisper.

All eyes on Terra now in anticipation. Her eyebrows knitted in confusion. How did they know, and should she say anything? Would it get Rosette in trouble? She stuffed a bite of the wrap thing in her mouth to avoid speaking. The minute the flavors hit her tongue she wished she hadn't done it. She grimaced in disgust.

Nalysse spoke, followed by giggles, "She has to be. She's eating elfin food and can't stand it."

"Most of us has a parent on the tribunal. There isn't anything they can keep from us. We live in the same home. We hear, but we don't discuss with anyone outside our circle here even other students whose parents are tribunal members," Kayln stated in her ever-decreasing quiet voice.

Terra didn't confirm or deny. She used her skills of avoidance to change the subject. "Nalysse called it. This thing is gross. What is it?"

Kinzo, who'd been quiet, answered her question, "It's an elfin dish and a favorite at the academy. Malp bulbs, tarroc, spee with teeple sprout dressing on the inside rolled into a bufoo leaf."

Terra lifted an eyebrow at him. "We need some other food here. I won't survive."

"And you're a hybrid? That's why you have rounded ears. Elf, fire-dragon, and something else?" Nalysse, Kinzo's girlfriend, piped in. "Hybrids don't exist. You're it."

Shifting in Terra's mind were several puzzle pieces; the infinity symbol on her chest, the door to the human realm, walking into Drakonia, human food, Tania, Tania again, and now why she had to disguise herself when everyone already knew. She couldn't help but wonder if Kinzo too had something to do with all of them knowing she was human and a hybrid.

"That's why I'm going to help you find that magic. You could have awesome powers none of us do. If anyone can help you reach them it's me." Meesha stood, towering over the table. Terra figured she was close to six feet tall. "Meet me after classes tomorrow and we'll talk with Gwond together."

10

Gwond's classroom was the last one in the hallway. It was large, with lavender sparkly paint like all the others. The floor tiled instead of wood. It lacked desks or furniture except the cubbies along the wall that held roll up mats.

He stood nearly two feet shorter than Meesha, with thick glasses, a beard that trailed over his pouchy belly, and a nearly bald head. His long tail, dark with green plumage on the end, that worked like an extra appendage. In class she'd seen other trolls and noted they were all short with tails.

"What can I do for my favorite student?" he asked, writing something on a pad of paper on top of the row of cubbies.

Meesha didn't mince words. "This is Terra. She's in your beginners' class on day four."

He put the pen down and strolled toward Terra then raked a hand through his dark colored beard as he studied her. "Yes, we can't have that." He glanced upwards at her behind his glasses. "You have a solution?"

"I do. You let me teach her."

His tail whipped around his leg. "We might be able to work something out."

Meesha had warned her trolls enjoyed bargaining and to let her do the talking. By the end of their negotiations, they sealed the deal. Meesha would train her and, twice a month, Terra would come by after class and demonstrate what she'd learned. It was a transaction Terra could live with.

Meesha insisted on learning in the woods behind the school. They sat in the grass, legs folded. "The first step in finding your magic is understanding who you are and how magic may manifest. There is predator and prey. Lycans, dragons, and vampires are predators. They are deadly, vicious, and should never be underestimated. Each has increased speed, agility, strength, and senses."

Terra listened as she explained the dynamics of each predator. Lycans shift into wolves and have wolf senses which make them good trackers on land. A wolf bite is venomous and kills vampires. It isn't more than a cold for a dragon but will cause harvesters and trolls to go crazy. The fae and elfin, if treated immediately, will recover fully but if not will suffer lifelong pain and infection at the location of the bite. They are social animals who thrive on the strength in their pack.

Vampires are their immortal enemies. Even though they live in cities, they are solitary creatures who live under the dictatorship of their Minister – the oldest vampire. Some shift into large cats, others have abilities that allow them to mind bend or wipe and others can portal. The older they get, the more skills they gain. The oldest vampires can do everything. Vampires track through blood, one sniff and they can find you beyond realm veils. One drop and they will always know where you are.

"The moral of the story: never let a vampire near your blood," Terra offered with a smile.

Meesha, who was always serious, said, "Never. It gets worse. They can drink commoner blood all day without adverse reactions, but pureblood from any other realm they get high."

In the Shadows

The image of a group of stoned vampires crossed Terra's mind and she chuckled.

Meesha's mouth curved into a smile. "It sounds silly but it's completely true. Vampires are known to portal to Lols for a fresh bite, time to time." She quickly followed up with, "They don't drain their prey and the venom in the bite heals it quickly and is supposed to feel good."

Terra wasn't horrified by the revelation. It gave her ideas. If vampires portalled to Lols maybe she could catch a ride or talk one into portalling her in. Hyacinth was a vampire. Did she portal?

Meesha got back on track. "Dragons are cousins of lycans and use echolocation in dragon form. Some breathe fire, others freeze water, and some shoot ice daggers from their mouths. Similar to lycans, they live in communities. They are excellent trackers in the air."

All this was interesting, but Terra didn't understand how any of it would help her reach in and discover her magic.

"Each has their weakness. Vampires can't face the sun. It is their final death. Dragons can't tolerate vampire blood and wolves lack an enzyme that tolerates silver. On the skin, silver burns a wolf; if ingested, it causes a painful death," Meesha explained, then paused, her eyes studying Terra's face.

"You are part dragon," she emphasized, "and may have predator abilities, but with elfin blood we don't know that for sure. Your powers could manifest in ways never seen. You need to know what to watch for."

Terra hadn't thought about it that way. There was still so much she didn't understand, but was anxious to see what those powers were.

Meesha pressed her back straight and blew out a deep breath. "Do what I do. Let go and release."

Following her lead, Terra breathed deeply and released several times. So far, she didn't feel any different.

Meesha stood and walked behind her. Keeping her voice even, she said, "Magic is all around you. In the air, the soil, and water beneath you. Allow it to enter through your pores, your breath. Hear it, feel it, see it. You are one."

Meesha's voice became quieter, sounding further away as Terra relaxed her entire being. Her arms dropping to her sides, her eyes shut, and breathing steady. Silence pervaded for several seconds as Terra's mind dropped into a void. A pulse pumped inside her, something she'd never noticed, yet it seemed familiar. Allowing herself to drown in the pulse, her senses became more acute and the rushing water of a brook pressed through her ears then a voice interrupted: *Terra.*

She popped her eyes open, irritated. *I'm in class, Rosette.* She hated the comicay and ripped it off her arm. She was there! She heard the water. She wanted to scream.

"Whoa, cool it. Wherever you were, you'll get back."

Terra blew out a long breath of frustration. "I heard the water beneath us. It was working."

Meesha, who'd sat sometime during Terra's trip into the magic unknown, scooted closer. "You'll find it again. What's important is what it tells us. You heard the water - that says you have increased hearing. A predator trait. We'll do more next week. In the meanwhile practice what I taught you and it'll come easier every time."

Meesha explained how her first power was hearing as well. It came and went, reminding Terra of the conversation she and Kinzo overheard the other day. Their voices loud, it caught her attention, then they drifted in and out. Was that the beginning?

"Tell me about Canida."

Meesha's lips pulled into a smile and she glanced over her shoulder towards the trees. "It's just over there," she said in a longing voice. "And it's beautiful. Green trees, mountains and forests. There're animals," she lifted her eyebrows, "everywhere."

"Sounds like my home. I lived in the city but we went camping and made off the grid trips. My dad liked the wilderness." Memories flooded her mind. She missed him.

"You want to see Canida?" Meesha said with an edge of excitement in her tone.

Heck yeah! Their desire for home was something they shared. Green trees, sunlight, water, and food. "Let's go." Terra jumped up.

Meesha's face twisted. "You can't go. I mean my memories. I show you mine, you show me yours."

Terra didn't have her cell phone with her and the comicay only tapped into memories when the device was on. Her life before here wasn't recorded in any device except her phone. "I can't. Those pictures aren't with me."

Meesha nodded her head. "I guess not."

Terra offered a hand. Meesha knitted her brows then accepted her offer and stood.

"I'm elfin, dragon, and something else. A mystery. If I'm lycan I can walk into Canida." She'd also marched into Drakonia but, as Kinzo assured her, vampires weren't fertile so it was impossible for her to be vampire. That night the mark appeared on her breast. What would it mean if she could open the curtain to Canida?

11

Canida was amazing and it hadn't taken much to convince Meesha to take her. She guessed she was as curious as Terra. What took convincing was getting her to take off the comicay.

Beyond the curtain, Terra saw the green field dotted in blue wildflowers, reminding her so much of her own realm. If she hadn't known she was in Canida, she'd have thought she was in Kansas, Colorado, or Wyoming. The tall grass of the green fields sprawled. A mountain range on the horizon.

Small, furry animals poked their heads through holes in the ground. Meesha called them poppers. They looked like jack rabbits to Terra, with their huge ears and slender faces. Flying insects that reminded her of something between a butterfly and dragonfly buzzed from flower to flower. The air smelled fresh and clean, unlike the horrid stench of Drakonia or even the eucalyptus-myrrh odor of Provence City.

She approached the curtain of Canida with more caution. Last time she literally ran into the curtain. This time she studied it, her eyes drawn to what she saw beyond. The pulse rising inside her as her eyes saw beyond the curtain. The mountains of Canida led to a high range to the left. She guessed that was Sier and to the right a dense forest of multi-colored trees. It reminded her of the memories Rosette shared of Aradia.

Curiouser were the markings on the curtain. She hadn't noted any before dropping it in Drakonia. Her eyes inspecting not rushing, the outline of a wolf head appeared like it was etched in glass. When she pressed her hands against the mark, molecules vibrated against her palms. Energy surged through her and the curtain simultaneously dissolved.

"You're lycan."

Terra shifted her eyes to Meesha whose face contorted with surprise before she lifted her elbow for a bump.

In the Shadows

"If you have enough lycan to drop the curtain to Canida then you shouldn't have a problem dropping it in Sier or Aradia?"

Meesha's words were more of a suggestion to Terra who stepped over the invisible barrier between Provence City and Canida. Kinzo wasn't able to see Drakonia after she broke the invisible plain, nor could he step into it. She wondered then what Meesha might see if she dropped the curtain to Sier.

Terra clutched her chest and curled in a ball beneath her covers. She'd expected the pain but wasn't prepared. Every labored breath tightened her chest, making it harder and harder and harder to catch her breath. She'd expected it, but wasn't physically or mentally prepared for it. That's why she hadn't suggested testing out her skills on Sier or Aradia. She didn't think she'd live through the carving of two or three marks at a time.

To lessen the pain, she focused on Halsey's snoring. It wasn't a heavy snore, but as Terra's mind centered on the nasal rattling it ramped up in decibels until her mind shifted to that instead of the excruciating pain in her chest.

Realm Walker

Fur tickled her leg as Clyde slunk up it and put his nose against her chest then curled into a ball. Small breaths from his tiny lungs sent warm air over the gouging pain and it decreased, one Clyde breath at a time.

Her last thoughts as sleep consumed her were of the map she'd drawn of the curtain. She used what she knew. Drakonia runs parallel to Aradia, noted when Kinzo showed her the moons. Canida was between them. Blood Falls connected Thraves and Drakonia. Verboten has freshwater streams that spill into the lavender seas of Navarrin. It was like the flag positions in the septagon room at Provence Academy. What she couldn't figure out was where Lols was located on that map.

By morning the mark hadn't appeared, but it didn't last time either. She hadn't noticed it until that night when she showered. She studied the food, remembering she'd found a blue fruit yesterday that tasted like mango and looked like a banana. She placed a couple on her tray then grabbed another couple fruit. One fuchsia, the other a seafoam color. If they tasted anything like the blue fruit she figured she could bring some to Tania who she planned on spending the day with since she didn't have classes.

She took a step back from the kiosk and turned on her heels, happy with her selection. Her tray hit a large woman. Her white hair so tightly pulled into a bun the sides of her face stretched with it. Hands on her hips in an unwelcoming fashion.

"No animals allowed!"

Terra's throat succumbed to an involuntary gulp at the woman's menacing size and enflamed words. It was one thing to stand up to Rosette but another to stand up to the woman in front of her, who could easily grab her by the throat and toss her across the room. She couldn't show any weakness. *I'm a predator,* she thought. Clyde wasn't any animal, he was hers. "He's my familiar and goes everywhere with me."

The woman's pinkish-blue eyes narrowed. "Not in my cafeteria!"

Her words rumbled the floor beneath Terra. Clyde burrowed his head into Terra's neck in fear. Terra squared her shoulders. She was fight in a smaller package. "We're leaving anyways!" Her head high, she walked past the woman and mumbled under her breath, "And your food sucks."

Silence pervaded and all eyes in the cafeteria stared at her as she made her way through the crowd to the outside table with her newly made friends.

"I can't believe how you stood up to her. She's an ice dragon with the personality of poison," Hyacinth stated as Terra took her seat.

"Elbow." Meesha raised hers for a bump which Terra obliged. "You and the predator are becoming one. I'm so proud of you but..." she raised a finger, "... be careful who you upset."

Nalysse, Caspen and Kayln chattered and praised her. The attention wasn't what she was seeking. She was merely standing up for Clyde who was small enough for the woman to squash like a bug.

"He's adorable," Nalysse offered, reaching a hand to tickle Clyde's head. He skirted down Terra's back and peeked his head between her and the back of the chair.

The conversation died down and everyone ran off to class. Only Terra and Hyacinth were left. Terra wasn't one to look past an opportunity, nor was she shy. She needed to get Tania back ASAP and felt the chance was worth it. Clyde approved of Hyacinth and she trusted him explicitly. "I hear vampires can portal to other realms. Is that true?"

12

It ended up that Hyacinth had an afternoon class then was going home for the weekend to Drakonia. Terra seized the opportunity. It turned out that Hyacinth herself wasn't a portaller. She shifted into a big cat. Proudly, she described herself as red with black stripes and triangles of black on her ears. All wasn't lost; her adopted brother was a portaller. That's how vampires did it – adoption – since they couldn't procreate on their own. She guessed being the living dead had its downfalls.

Terra opened up that the portal wasn't for her alone but someone else. She had to trust her. It was Meesha who told her vampires were lone creatures and, with Clyde's approval, she had to trust her. There wasn't another option. She'd hoped Kinzo would come up with a suggestion, but he hadn't and was too busy with Nalysse. Tania was her responsibility.

Hyacinth cringed as they neared the portable. It was the equivalent of a cat hackling its fur to scare someone off. Terra chuckled inside. Vampires being the immortal enemies of lycans, it made sense. She was beginning to understand a lot of things.

Tania sat at the kitchen table when they entered. Hyacinth, as if forgetting she was in the enemy's home, said, "It's true. Another commoner!" Her brown eyes opened wide. "You're the one they are looking for. We have to get you out of here. Hiding in here is clever though, I'll give you that."

A smile curved Tania's lips as though she got it. Cats and dogs don't mix. "It was cool at first, being here, you know but it's gotten old. There's nothing here and I miss," she glanced at Terra as apologizing for her next words, "home and school."

Terra understood completely. She only wished she could go back with her.

Hyacinth clapped her hands against her cheeks. "You have to understand this is dangerous. All the vamps and harvesters are looking for you, including students, especially students. I won't say anything. The secret is safe with me and my brother will help. He doesn't mind breaking a rule or two, but we have to do this secretly."

She tented her hands on the table. "You see, you were supposed to have died and been harvested. Somehow you escaped that. The vampires and harvesters have kept this from the tribunal. If they'd have said something everyone would be on lock down, but we aren't. I guess they figured a young woman wouldn't be that difficult to find. The next tribunal meeting is Monday. This has to be done before that and with you *missing* there will be extra guards at the Drakonia border."

"I was meant to die in that cave?" Tania asked, her beautiful face twisted in shock.

Oops! Maybe Terra should have said something, but what did she know? She was a stranger as much as Tania.

Hyacinth nodded as she winced. "I'm sorry."

Tania leaned back. "If I go back, will I live since, you know, my time was…?" her voice drifted off.

"Maybe it wasn't your time. You did survive," Terra offered, to soothe her friend. She didn't know. If she went back, would her time be up and the harvesters come again? Would she continue her life? The thought of them coming after her to fix their mistake was harsh. It wasn't something she wanted for her but, if she stayed here, no doubt they'd find her. She shuddered at the thought of what would happen if they did. Going home to Lols was the best option.

"This hasn't happened before, not as far as I know. Sometimes fledglings mess up but this is big. I don't even know how you escaped Drakonia." Hyacinth turned to Terra. "I don't get how you were able to enter Drakonia… I guess maybe since you're both commoners you could have an ancestor that is vampire. That might allow you passage. This is uncharted waters. All of it."

Hyacinth left for class, promising to talk with her brother that day and asked them to meet her and her brother on the hill on Sunday. Terra remembered how Kinzo took her there the first time they hung out. He showed her the moons. The next day they, or rather she, found Tania.

Terra spent the afternoon with Tania. Their time was short and every second counted. She was happy, yet stressed a little. All the things that could go wrong circling in her head. What if they got caught? What if they couldn't get back into Drakonia? Could they trust Hyacinth's brother? What if the portal fell apart? She didn't know the first thing about how portals worked other than what she'd seen in urban fantasy movies. Were real portals the same? Kinzo said he saw a swirling teal mass before she walked over the barrier between Provence and Drakonia. Was that a portal?

Tania ate the fruit she brought her. She guessed even stressed she was starving. There wasn't much to eat. More than anything she wanted to go back with her. Return to her life, only it wouldn't be the same without her father.

They talked for the next couple hours. It helped ease their apprehensions. Tania was from New York, although not a native. She'd moved there from Georgia when she was ten. She was currently a second year at NYU. Like Terra, she missed the crowded streets and city lights. She'd taken up spelunking when she was fifteen, enjoying the adventure of discovering something hidden from the rest of the world. She chuckled, "I didn't know there were entire hidden realms."

"Me either," Terra responded. She guessed the adventure and "hidden world" was the reason Tania had taken so quickly to Provence. The weight of homesickness and trepidation lingered on her words now. At first Terra thought she'd have to force her home. Not anymore; she was ready.

Curious herself if the mark she felt burning into her last night had inked, Terra pulled her shirt down. Glancing at it upside down she couldn't see anything, but Tania claimed there was a light outline forming of a wolf head. She traced it at the two o'clock position. According to her map, that was correct, or rather her map was correct. Either way.

Terra pulled her shirt up, enjoying the linger of Tania's finger more than she should. Afterall, she was going home. Their eyes met briefly before Clyde interrupted them.

He jumped between their feet then bobbed near the front door as if wanting to go outside and explore. When Terra clasped the doorknob to open the door he ran and hid under a bed. "What is it?"

The ferret peeked his masked face out from under the mattress then turned, going further under the bed. He only did that when he was scared. Instead of using her human senses and pushing the curtain aside, which might give them away, she used her predator senses and pressed her ear against the door and listened. Remembering her lesson with Meesha she let go, becoming one with the surrounding energy. Voices rang through her ears. Her heart quickened, rushing blood through her veins. 'Nothing's been spotted here and the place smells like dog,' said a man. Another chuckled at the comment. Footfalls moved away from the portable.

She turned and rested against the door. A smile on her face. Tania's wide, golden-brown eyes inspected Terra. "A couple of vampires, I think, but they're gone."

Hyacinth hadn't liked the odor either. Her reaction still fresh in Terra's mind. "You're safe in here if no one sees you. Vampires are repelled by wolves and this place housed at least four." That's what Hyacinth meant when she said it was smart to hide her there.

Tania dropped her head. "As much as I want to return, there's so much here I haven't explored… My parents, though, are paying a fortune for my education. If I don't return, it'll be a waste of their money."

Rushing to her side, Terra scooted onto the edge of the bed near her. Was that really all she was worried about? "Listen, it'll work out and you'll have access to decent food again." They both chuckled.

Tania raised her head. "Yeah, it's hard to live on fruit and jerky alone."

"I'll miss you." Terra placed a hand on Tania's. They had two more nights. In that time they had exploring to do. That was it. She'd take her to Sier, or at least try. Tania liked to spelunk and Sier was the highlands. There had to be caves. "Tonight, we'll visit a realm while we still have the chance."

13

Unfortunately, Halsey was in the room, radiating negativity and entitlement, when Terra returned. "Where do you always go?"

Terra ignored her as she opened a textbook to read. She was learning more by exploration, but it might serve to fend off Halsey. As a hybrid, she was different than everyone else. She wondered if Tania could open any curtains. Tonight would be the night to find out. She was sure she could, as her dad was a dragon; certainly Sier wouldn't be a problem. She had more dragon than lycan which would be mixed with elf, and opened that one without problems.

Halsey sighed loudly. "Are you going to the elfin party in Aradia tomorrow night?"

That caught Terra's attention. She hadn't heard anything about it. If she was to play elfin, why hadn't anyone told her? She felt betrayed by Kinzo. The stab hurt like Halsey meant it to but she refused to let it show, confirming she'd said anything that affected her.

"They do it every year. I hear it's a blast."

Heat rose in Terra's cheeks. *Easy Terra.* In her best nonchalant tone she responded while turning a page. She wasn't about to look at her in case her flushed cheeks gave Halsey any satisfaction. "I'm thinking about it," she countered.

Halsey stood in front of a mirror, primping her hair. "Maybe you can take him too," she stated, meaning Clyde.

Every word from the fae's mouth grated like metal on metal on her nerves. She refused to give Halsey the satisfaction. "Any parties in Navarin?"

"We're fae. We don't do pointless teenage parties," she huffed.

We don't do pointless teenage parties, she repeated in her head. *You mean you aren't invited, Queen Bee.* "Then why are you tossing clothes on your bed?"

"If you were here more often you'd know I always do this. A Diama has to look

stunning every day. I represent the crown."
Terra caught the obvious eye-roll.

Sooo glad I'm not fae. "I have studying to do." She grabbed her book and Clyde. She wouldn't get anything done with the fae-wench around.

In the library, she snuggled into a large, cozy velvet chair and worked on her map. The librarian agreed to let Clyde join her. In fact, she seemed taken with him and he with the bright purple plumage of her tail.

Her map was coming along as she added details to it and made notes of what she'd learned so far. Was it possible she was lycan and vampire? That was two opposing forces. She glanced at the shelves of books. Was there anything in the library about hybrids? With the million or so books lining the walls, there had to be something.

From the corner of her eye she spotted a girl who looked about fifteen, maybe sixteen, a few velvet chairs away. When Terra turned her head the girl immediately dropped her eyes to her book. She tucked a chunk of cyan hair behind her ear, drawing attention to it. Elves had long pointy ears, fae had more humanlike, shorter ears with pointy tips. This girl had medium ears with points unlike Terra's rounded tips.

Her shoulder-length hair a striking lilac with seafoam green, cyan, and brown chunks. She learned not all fae had blonde hair, only some land fae like Halsey who were extra privileged because they shifted into unicorns. She didn't get why that was so special. Did other fae not shift? Was the girl full fae? She was very self-conscious about the hybrid thing since she was the only one.

The girl lifted an eye again and, noting Terra was staring at her, diverted her attention to the book in her lap. Terra had gotten used to awkward glances in the human realm. She had hazel eyes and skin depending on her surroundings. In Provence City, others weren't sure what to make of her. If Terra was anyone else, she may have felt awkward for staring at the girl, but the girl started it. She was studying her. She grabbed the handle to Clyde's harness and plopped into the seat next to the girl who shifted her eyes from the book and met Terra's. "I'm Terra."

"Cat."

She had some tact and didn't come straight out with her thoughts. "I'm in need of a book that has certain information. Do you spend much time here?"

The girl dropped the book in her lap and gave Terra her full attention. "Sometimes. I like to read."

"I couldn't help but notice your ears. Not in a bad way," she corrected herself and turned her head to display her profile. "See, mine are rounded."

The girl touched her ears as if wanting to hide them or embarrassed by them.

"No, I like them. They're different." She was doing her best to beat around the bush and filter but wasn't sure the girl was understanding.

Then Cat's blue-green eyes lit up. "I think I know a book."

The four-foot-nothing troll librarian with purple plumage on her tail strolled towards Terra. The slacks of her pants swishing together. The sound was almost deafening to Terra. *I need to learn to control that.* Now that she'd unlocked some magic, she didn't have a way to shut it off.

"Terra O'Malley?" the librarian asked as Terra nodded her head. Her gut twisting with the idea she might be in trouble, but for what she had no idea. "You're wanted in Dean Salena's office."

Why were her instincts right this time? Ugh! She may have met the first hybrid besides herself. Disappointment overwhelmed her. "Nice to meet you, Cat."

Her walk to the Dean's office was fraught, but not with concern over what kind of trouble she might be in. She doubted they knew anything about her trip to Drakonia or Canida or had any clue about Tania. On the other hand, over-confidence wasn't always a redeeming quality, especially when one was on the way to the Dean's office.

She followed the hallway to the center. Up the floating staircase were the classes, behind the stairs was the septagonal room, but where exactly was the office? She'd been there on day one to get her schedule, but wasn't sure now. She didn't have the map with her. She glanced at the comicay on her arm. Rosette went over its many uses, like communications, saving and sharing memories, as well as finding places. GPS or the Provence equivalent.

She pressed the middle and thought: *Take me to the Dean's office.* A map only she could see spread out in front of her. That was pretty awesome. Cell phones didn't quite do that, nor could you simply think something into them. She stepped forward, following an arrow that appeared when she moved, made a left down a short hallway and into the main office area.

A lycan, judging by her tall size and slender, muscled figure, glanced up and placed the pen in her hand on the desk. "Terra. Dean Salena is waiting for you."

Terra curved her lips into the best fake smile she could. "Thanks." It wasn't the secretary's fault and the Dean was a fae.

The woman's eyes drifted to Clyde as he scampered alongside Terra who was busy noting the woman didn't have a chair and thinking how awful to stand all day. She pushed the cracked door open. Dean Salena's back was to her, facing the window. She had quite a view of the courtyard and gardens.

As she turned, Terra watched her ears closely. Without a doubt they were more humanlike and smaller than Cat's. Darn! She'd have to find her again. If she was a book worm, the library was her best bet.

Her mauve eyes dropped to Clyde who sniffed around her room. "Take a seat."

Dropping into one of the plush purple chairs across from Salena's desk, she noted how comfy they were and wondered why the secretary didn't have one. *Is it above her pay grade?* Even in Lols where others were banished, secretaries had chairs. Completely distracted, Terra didn't pay much attention as Salena strode behind her desk until the clicking of her heels against the wood floor pounded against her eardrums.

Salena placed her hands on her desk and leaned forward. "I agreed with Rosette to allow the pet. I was hoping it would help you acclimate to the school but…" there it was, the but, always a but, "… you can't pick fights with Matilda."

Who? She'd met a few people, but a Matilda wasn't one of them.

As if reading her expression or maybe her mind, she dropped gently into the chair behind her desk. "Matilda is the lead food service engineer."

Terra's eyes widened. The ice dragon! "She started it, by picking on Clyde. She's an adult, I'm a kid," the words hurled from her mouth. "There's no sign that says ferrets or other animals aren't allowed and he's my familiar. Wherever I go, he goes." Terra clasped her arms around her chest with a sneer. She figured no one in Provence or any other realm even knew what a familiar was.

Clyde hopped into the chair next to Terra, stood on his hind legs and pressed his front paws on the desk then hissed. Salena tented her hands and glanced at him then Terra. She snubbed him. "He's not allowed."

"Fine. I'll starve! The food is crap anyways. Not once have I seen anything human on that menu. Yes, I know you know I'm playing elf but I'm really human or a 'commoner'," she said, using air quotes. She wasn't done. "You can do one better and portal me home where I can eat all the burritos and Applewood smoked bacon cheeseburgers I want!"

The chair tilted as Salena leaned back. "You want us to provide you with commoner food?"

"Yes."

She tapped her fingers together. "We do provide blood types warm, cold, or shaken for the vampires, so we may be able to work something out, but the animal has to stay out of the cafeteria. It's a sterile environment and nobody wants to eat a hair of his that fell into their food."

When was the last time she visited the cafeteria? It wasn't sterile. Like any school cafeteria it contained children breathing and spitting water droplets from their mouths every time they opened them. "Clyde needs food too. He's a carnivore." She was pushing it. "He likes kitten food but the vet sells pellets that contain more complete nutrition." She was running low, as he ate several times a day. Clyde dropped his paws from the desk and sniffed the air.

"And pet food." She leaned forward in her chair. "Why don't you make a list and we'll see what we can do."

Really? That was it? Yes, it was. She dismissed her in time for dinner, more blue mango-like fruit. If this kept up, she'd never eat mango again. *Take me to the courtyard,* she thought to her comicay.

The cafeteria, normally crowded, was much thinner. It was day 5 and they could go home for the weekend. She told Rosette this morning she was staying at the school. Rosette didn't seem to mind or try and talk her in to coming home. If she had to guess, Rosette was glad to be home alone and not have someone there to bother her.

Nalysse and Kinzo were absent for dinner. That was for the better. Not being invited to an elf party in Aradia when every other elf would be there stung like a wasp. Caspen and Hyacinth were absent. She knew Hyacinth was going home and figured maybe Caspen was too. She sighed. The elf party was tomorrow. No doubt they headed home to Aradia. She sighed heavily.

Kayln smiled as Terra took her seat. "Here," she handed a blue fruit to Terra.

"Thanks," she responded. It was as if she'd read her mind. Maybe she had, and it was a fae thing.

Meesha dropped her tray on the table and slid into her seat. "Done any practice today?" She opened a packet and sprinkled it on the steaming meat dish on her plate. She thought of the prairie bunnies or poppers and wondered what kind of animal Meesha was eating.

"Some. My hearing comes and goes. Sometimes quiet noises become overwhelming, like my roommate snoring."

Kayln snorted then covered her mouth.

Terra chuckled too, then pointed out: "I'm not fae. I don't have to like her or be nice."

"She's awful. I don't think she has a single true friend," Kayln responded in a quiet voice to avoid Halsey or one of her "ladies" overhearing.

For a split second she felt sympathy for the dreadful fae-wench then spotted her in the center of the cafeteria barking orders at the females flittering around her like butterflies, and sympathy was replaced with disgust.

Kayln sighed. "I admire the sky fae. They're so colorful," she said in longing. Her eyes fixed in Halsey's direction.

"Your vision may spaz too until you learn to control it. Eating pikos isn't going to help. As a predator, you need meat in your diet. Prey can live off fruit and vegetables but not predators." Meesha pushed her plate. "Take a bite."

Peer pressure, plain and simple. She gulped, hoping the meat wasn't from a cute furry little animal and picked up the bite Meesha cut away for her. It felt and looked like steak. She pushed the bite into her mouth and chewed. It wasn't steak. The taste was tangy and sweet yet juicy, with the texture of beef. With steak sauce it might be edible. She swallowed and hoped it didn't give her the runs later.

14

"**W**hat do you see?" Terra asked Tania as they stood feet from the curtain between Provence City and Sier.

"Not much, it's dark." She squinted her eyes. "Mountains maybe, and an outline of a wing or winged animal."

Through the darkness, Terra spotted high mountains, a golden moon, billions of stars, and a clear outline of a dragon on the curtain. She did have predator blood and Tania was human. From what she could tell, humans were hybrids but, after centuries of evolution, she guessed those skills lessened each generation. Rosette admitted magical creatures lost their magic almost immediately when they entered Lols. "Try pressing your hands against the wing."

She figured since Tania could see beyond the curtain, even if not very well, she could maybe dissolve the curtain.

Tania lifted her hands and carefully pressed her palms against the wing of the dragon image. It didn't immediately vanish like curtains did for Terra, so maybe Tania wasn't a dragon. That was OK, but she could see. All this was fresh to her. Possibly it took a certain amount of dragon to bring down the curtain. Someone, she couldn't remember who, mentioned something like that.

"Do you feel the energy vibrating against your palms?"

"No." Tania dropped her hands. "It's not working for me."

The disappointment in her voice tugged at Terra. "We'll do it together." She stood behind Tania, wove her fingers through Tania's and leaned forward, Tania's back against Terra's chest, her face against her neck. She smelled delicious. Terra fought the urge to kiss her supple neck.

The attraction between them seemed to go both ways, as she'd felt something from Tania earlier in the day and now, pressed against her, she felt her pulse quicken.

They pressed together against the curtain. Energy bubbled and bounced. "Do you feel that?"

In the Shadows

"I do," her words breathy.

Terra fought her hormonal urges as the curtain evaporated and they dropped their hands. Terra let go of Tania's for a second as she walked to her side and enclosed her left around Tania's and squeezed. "Are you ready?"

"Let's do it."

They stepped across the plain together, no problems. It took energy to break the curtain. The energy felt slightly different between Sier and Canida. Sier was more effervescent. It felt like uncorking a bottle of champagne, which she'd done the past few New Years with her father. Drakonia was such a surprise she didn't remember. It wasn't like she'd meant to walk into a see-through magic curtain.

The golden moon was the color of Tania's eyes. In Sier it shed more light than behind the curtain, illuminating snowy-capped mountains. They stood on a narrow plateau worn by the weather, about four feet in width. It stretched towards the side of a tall mountain that extended into the clouds. Frozen wind chilled them to the bone. Luckily, Terra had brought them each a sweater to wear.

Clyde's harness was looped around Terra's arm as he perched on her shoulder. He wrapped himself into her neck for warmth.

"New York is cold, but this is below freezing. I feel like I'm in Antarctica," Tania said between chattering teeth. "I think I see a cave. It'll be warmer."

Terra felt Tania's excitement bubble through their clasped hands as she stepped alongside her, the cave entrance barely visible. It appeared as a black spot on the mountain that filled in as they neared. The oval entry small, they had to duck. Once inside, Tania turned on the flashlight of her phone, illuminating the creamy, rocky walls of the narrow passage.

The slender path led to a larger cavern with smoother walls and one exit on the other side. The air noticeably warmer, they began to thaw. Tania, the cave expert, paused as she shone her light into the dark passage, showing its steep decline. They sat on their butts and scooted downhill.

Energy pulsed through Terra's palms from the stone floor. A familiar feeling overwhelmed her and she pulled her hands off the floor, attempting to scoot with only her legs and feet. She'd never been to Sier, not that she recalled. Initially recoiling from the deja vu, she remembered Meesha's words that energy was everywhere. It wasn't something she should fear, but welcome.

Closing her eyes, she focused on the energy and the pulse pumping inside her, connecting her to magic, and let the visions enter her mind. It wasn't her hearing this time but vision — a map. It was rudimentary, filled with lines and paths. Beneath them, another cavern with several exits, some of the paths meandered with others shooting off while others led to larger caverns. One could get really confused. When she reached the bottom she focused her energy, keeping sight of the map.

Tania spun in circles. "Look at this place. I've never seen anything quite like it." Excitement beaming from her like golden energy.

Crystals sparkled in the walls as Tania shone her flashlight across them. Streaks of metal were embedded in the smooth rock. Much deeper in the cave was a never-ending series of tunnels and caverns.

"If we go left, there's a large cavern. I think it's a city. The path straight has a deep drop, but also leads to a large cavern," Terra said.

Tania placed a hand on her hip, her eyes exploring the walls of the cave. "How do you know that?"

Terra shrugged. "I can see it like a map. The cavern to the left is massive and the dragons live in the caves to the right, so it makes sense."

"Who says they live in caves?"

"I do. My father was a dragon." She knew instinctively, letting the magic guide her.

"If we go left there's a platform above it." He didn't really live in a cave, or if he had he'd never told her.

"OK." Tania shrugged. "I'm game." Her voice bubbly with excitement and adventure.

"So, what's your thing with caves?" Terra asked, genuinely curious. She'd told her earlier, but Terra wanted to hear it again.

Tania stepped into the passageway. "They're hidden worlds beneath the surface carved by weather and water and each is as unique as the life that lives in them. Look at the walls, how smooth they are, and the crystals and metals in the cavern. I'm sure you won't find those anywhere on Earth, maybe not even deeper into this cave."

The decline wasn't steep, which is why Terra thought this was the better path. She focused hard on the mind map. The magic stuff was new to her. Pressing her hands against the wall energized it and showed her more details like rooms. No, not rooms… more like apartments. She paused as the realization hit her and tapped Tania on the shoulder.

Tania turned around. "What?"

In a low voice Terra whispered, "I think we're surrounded by dragons." She pointed to the left. "There's a door, and ahead about a mile maybe is another door. It's like this is the country and the cavern is the city."

In the Shadows

Tania pressed her hands against her cheeks, her eyes wide. "Maybe we'll see one," she said, attempting to keep her voice quiet despite her excitement.

It seemed they'd walked a couple miles and passed several doors by the time they reached the ledge over the large cavern. Light radiated from the sizable crystals sprinkled in the walls, drawing attention to the many doors behind carved ledges.

There must have been thousands with numbers and words carved into the stone beside them. She couldn't make out the words. Inaudible voices drifted into her ears, catching her off guard, drawing her attention to the people below. Not many, but enough. "Duck." Dragons were predators, which meant they had crazy extreme vision and hearing.

Tania glanced at her as Terra lowered herself, pressing her back against the wall. She sat beside her. "This place is bigger than all of Provence. I bet hundreds of thousands of dragons live here."

Terra tilted her head toward Tania in explanation. How would Tania know the size of Provence if she was staying inside the portable with the green curtains drawn and out of sight of vampires and others?

"I've done some exploring. It's boring being cooped in the mobile home. I've been careful," she iterated, knowing Terra wouldn't approve.

"You can't do that. If you get caught—"

Tania interrupted, "I won't. Like I said, I'm careful. I certainly won't now that I know they're looking for me. I'm too young to die. I need a second chance… There're a lot of woods. It's mostly woods." She paused. "I can't get through the curtains though, at least any I tried. I didn't know how until today, but I've tried touching some, searched for buttons, eye scanners, everything. I can't get in."

Being stuck in the portable, or mobile home as she called it, was probably boring in the extreme. She didn't blame her for getting out and exploring. Given the same circumstances, Terra would probably do the same. What caught her attention the most was that Tania could enter realms but couldn't open curtains. Was her genetics, or blood, or whatever it was that allowed the curtains to drop, not enough? If it wasn't enough, how could she walk in the realms?

Her dad a dragon, walking into Sier made sense. Her mom being part elf, and something else she assumed was lycan, she couldn't be 50% of either. Maybe at least 25%? "There's a party tomorrow in Aradia. I wasn't invited." It burned her up the elves didn't ask her to attend, especially Kinzo. He was the first friend she'd made. He hadn't even visited Tania. What reason could they have? "I say we crash it."

Tania's golden-brown eyes lit up like the crystals in the cave. "Absolutely." Tania held her palm out for a pump.

Meesha entered Provence. She needed a run and chasing poppers was always a hoot. She never caught them, harmed them, or ate them. It was a game, and lycans today were civilized, unlike their ancestors. The idea of raw meat wasn't appetizing to her in the least.

Her wolf senses still alert, two female voices beamed into her head. Glancing in their direction, she spotted Terra and another girl with longer, brown hair leaving Sier. She didn't recognize the other girl. Using lycan stealth, she followed them without so much as the crack of a small branch. Their conversation focused on the caves in Sier.

The girl could be elf, but certainly not dragon. The dark hair gave that away. Fire dragons were gingers and ice dragons white-haired. She was neither. Nosy wasn't her best quality, but what good was it to have keen senses if she never used them?

They entered the mobile unit left in Provence by the lycans. It was one of many used when they built the city. Lycan logic dictated they leave it in case repairs were ever needed. She'd completely forgotten about it, as it was buried deep in the woods between Thraves and Sier.

Their focus shifted from caves and dragons to the elfin party. Not an elf, she'd never been interested, but understood how Terra would be as she was at least part elf. It surprised Meesha the other elves hadn't invited her. That was a huge slight.

She stayed in her position, fighting the urge to get closer, even join them. Terra had explaining to do, but stealth often dictated spying over outright confrontation. The girls were planning on crashing the party. Unable to join them, Meesha planned on following them tomorrow night and waiting. She'd catch them upon their exit.

Her curiosity about the girl who clearly was a hybrid, or even a commoner, deserved answers.

15

Bane and Metford

The wall behind Bane was a deep magenta. Metford always assumed vampires liked lots of color because it reminded them of life before death. His dark hair slicked back, mustache styled to perfection, and tailored suit; Bane always looked impeccable. He bet the dress shoes on his feet shone as well. "We have concluded our search. She's vanished as far as we can tell."

"We may have a lead," Bane said, leaning back in a fine elfin-weave fabric chair. "In Provence City. We aren't sure where she's been hiding, but have set up a situation to "portal" her home."

Nobody was portalling her anywhere, except Traves. That's where she belonged.

The accident that should have claimed her life went horribly wrong. It wasn't their doing, the veil was too thin and the fledgling too inexperienced, but her soul was past due for Tranquility. The veil between Thraves and other realms was as it needed to be to harvest but it was thinning more each day. "When will this meeting occur?"

"Sunday... Day 7. She will be brought to Drakonia."

Metford knew Bane well. Even in a holocall between realms when they weren't physically face to face he could tell when he was hiding something. "I need to have people ready to accept her. What is the plan?"

Bane lifted one leg over the other. "We've been keeping tabs on comicay footage and discovered one of our youths offering to portal someone into Lols."

He understood what that meant. The stowaway, as Metford had come to think of her, hadn't discovered the portal to Lols in Provence City. It was hidden well and kept under lock and key. They couldn't have humans coming and going as they pleased. Vampires were expert portallers who used their skill to make visits to the human realm. Whoever was helping her knew that. Level 3 magic wasn't allowed, or possible, in Provence City which meant they were bringing her back to Drakonia. Metford tugged his goatee. "And you think it's her."

"Yes. Who else would want to go to Lols?"

He could think of one other. "Could it be the new girl who came from Lols? She could be homesick." She was a kid and Provence City, he imagined, was a lot for a young commoner to adjust to.

"We've thought of that, but don't think that's it. She'd be missed," he said, referring to her aunt.

He didn't want Bane to think he had any power in the situation. He also bet Bane had little to do with what happened to her. M'ra seemed to run a tight ship and have a leash attached to every vampire. "We will have a team ready to accept her to Thraves."

"What about our other problem?" Bane asked.

Cyrus's soul was never harvested, which meant one of two things: he never died; or he went to the Otherworld. Harvested souls went to Tranquility where he guessed they lived in utopia, other souls not worthy went to the Otherworld – an unpleasant, lonely place. Harvesters weren't allowed in Tranquility and the gatekeepers refused any information. They were stoic.

Over the years, special teams were sent to the Otherworld. None there recalled Cyrus. He vanished the day of the cleansing – quite literally. The team sent last week hadn't uncovered anything new, or anything on the girl. "The team hasn't found anything different. We will leave them there until the girl is returned." It wasn't much of a card to play. He sighed internally.

He didn't think they'd find anything between now and three days from now but, being a diplomat, it was about give and take. The vampires would think they were searching. Metford liked Cyrus. At the time he was only a fledgling trainer. He'd hit it off with Cyrus who was so filled with questions. If only he'd understood those questions were to build his power. The more he understood of each realm the stronger he got. Cyrus had used him and let him down, yet he still liked him. He could have brought down all the realms, but he didn't. That, to Metford, showed restraint.

Bane twirled his chair, meeting Metford's gaze for a moment. "We will be in touch."

The holo image vanished and Metford was alone in his office. He stood and padded to the window carved into the stone walls. His first office as a fledgling trainer had a horrible view. It faced the backside of Blood Falls. This one was more pleasant, as he looked towards the snow-capped peaks of the mid-lands. He preferred home over Provence City and spent more time in it.

16

Terra awoke Saturday curled against Tania. It was late when they returned from their adventure in Sier. Aware and expectant, she knew she'd get a new mark, one that matched the dragon imprinted on the curtain. She wasn't sure about Tania. In an effort to save her the pain, they curled in bed with Clyde between them.

It was his warm breath that took her pain away when the wolf head inked into her chest. It worked again, the two of them slept soundly through the night. If the mark inked into her she hadn't felt it.

Returning to the school, she put Clyde in her backpack and zipped it, promising to take him out once they left the cafeteria. Glancing at the menus brought its normal dismay. There was something that looked similar to a fluffy biscuit. She grabbed two, then fruit. Plenty of fruit. She was feeding herself and Tania. It was more important now than ever that Tania didn't leave the portable and she felt she understood that.

She didn't bother to sit at the table, but found a spot under a tree outside the courtyard so Clyde could run and play while she ate. The courtyard was surrounded by trees and flowering bushes. Small birds flitted from branch to branch. Sinking her teeth into the biscuit thing, it wasn't bad. It wasn't as sweet as the biscuits from Lols, nor as fluffy, but it was bread – bland bread.

Returning to her room, she crossed her fingers as she opened the door in hopes Halsey wasn't there. Sighing relief when she entered an empty room, she opened the middle drawer of her dresser in search of her hat. If she and Tania were crashing the elf party, Tania needed a disguise to cover her round ears.

Strapping Clyde's harness on him, the door opened. The fae-wench stood in the doorway. Terra's face and body visibly cringed.

Halsey's beautiful features twisted in displeasure. "Where have you been?"

In the Shadows

Like it was her business. "I went home last night to see my aunt in Provence, not that you deserve any explanation." It was quick thinking, and Halsey didn't deserve an explanation, but she also didn't need her spoiling any plans.

She harrumphed. It was very unbecoming for a *Diama*. "You must be attending the party tonight. Is that why you returned?"

The party wasn't here, but in Aradia. She was the nosiest, most useless and annoying fae she'd met. "I gotta run. An elf's life is always an adventure." She was out the door before the fae-wench could get out another word.

She hadn't left the campus when she spotted Cat. The hybrid from the library. She was sitting on a bench beneath a large shade tree, its lavender leaves spread above her. Terra debated. Did she stop and talk with her again, or get to Tania? Likely she was starving and waiting for Terra.

When Cat raised her head and glanced Terra's way she took that as a welcome sign in glowing neon letters. Cat's head returned to the book and Tania sat down beside her. It was a conversation she felt needed to happen. In all of Provence Academy she hadn't met one other hybrid.

Terra sat on the bench beside her. The teal of the sky shining against Cat's blue chunks. "I know we only just met, but your ears…" There she went with the ears again. "Are you part elf?" She spat it out, unfiltered and completely Terra-like.

Cat lifted her head from the book and stared at Terra in shock with her wide blue-green eyes.

Sensing her fear and discomfort at the topic, Terra toned it down. "I'm sorry. I haven't met anyone like me at the school and I thought. maybe since we have it in common. we could… be friends… or at least talk about it."

Cat glanced around the area and, in a quiet voice, said, "We could get in trouble for talking about it."

Terra ripped her comicay off. "Not if they don't know."

Cat giggled then ripped hers off too. Terra took that as a sign that she felt as out of place as she did. Finally, someone she had something in common with besides Tania who she was helping covertly send home and crossing her fingers the harvesters wouldn't find her again.

"I'm part elf, part dragon too, and I think part lycan. I have to pretend. I hate it. I just want to be me. When I saw you the other day we connected on a level I haven't with anyone else. They don't know what it's like to be a hybrid. It shouldn't be a bad word." The sentences rolled off Terra's tongue.

In the Shadows

In a quiet voice, as if someone might overhear, Cat responded, "I know. I'm mostly fae, not much elf. I've been pretending all my life but when I…" she paused.

Terra waited expectantly. Her eyes asking: *When you what?*

"You have to promise, no jokes," Cat insisted.

What joke could Terra possibly have? "I pinky swear." She held out her pinky. Cat gawked at her strangely, then the light bulb clicked and she got it, bringing her pinky to Terra's.

"I'm a water fae. We shift into mermaids and mermen, but I shift into a catfish," she said the last word under her breath.

The joke pushed through her brain. Cat who turns into a catfish. Terra imagined the *'Is your last name fish?'* got pretty old. She stifled her chuckle. "That's cool! I don't have any special skills yet." Then it dawned on her Cat was part elf. She bet she wasn't invited to the party either. "There's an elf party in Aradia tonight. You want to crash it with me?"

"No." Cat shook her head in near horror. "I mean, no I'm going home today for the weekend. My parents are expecting me."

It didn't appear anyone was expecting her or that she had anywhere to actually go, but didn't push it. Talking with her was enough and she did appear a bit shy. The other fae were so snooty, except Kayln – and she was bubble-headed. At first she'd been annoying, but she'd warmed to her. Cat was far friendlier. The rejection wasn't personal, she figured. She did have one more question: "Hey, umm… about that book."

Cat giggled. "It's in the ancient texts section, under S for Spells and Magic. There's an entire section in the book on hybrids. I don't think anyone knows except me, otherwise it wouldn't be there."

"Thanks!" Terra stood. "Maybe we can talk more."

Cat nodded. Her seafoam-cyan hair flowing with the movement. "I'd like that."

17

The curtain between Provence and Aradia was a softer energy, like a cat's content purr. Tania and Terra paused inside the curtain. Aradia glowed. Surrounding the trees were flowers that glowed like neon sapphires. The air buzzed with tiny creatures lit in every color. Clyde bounded forward, leaping into the air after the tiny dots of color.

"Wow!" Tania mouthed. "There's beauty in caves but this is unreal like a fairy tale."

"An elf tale." Terra chuckled at her own joke.

"Either or," Tania said with a smile. "Clyde's found new playmates," she noted as the ferret bounded and leapt into the air.

Terra chuckled. "Let's follow him," she suggested, strolling toward the silly animal.

More attuned to her magic, she relaxed her body, allowing the energy to surge into her. She was about to test the long-hair elf belief. Focusing on the plants, she asked in her mind: *Guide us to the party.* A gust of wind blew against their backs, pushing their hair forward. Terra pushed the hair from her face and watched the direction of the leaves.

Clyde was heading in the right direction, if the wind and leaves were a message from the trees. She liked to think it was, and the whole thing about long hair was an urban myth. The flora and branches were so dense she only managed to see small parts of the sky. The tiny bugs flew past her face so quick she couldn't make them out. "Do you think they are pixies?"

"What?"

"The glowing, flying things."

Tania chuckled. "No, they're like lightning bugs only in different colors."

Terra wasn't familiar with lightning bugs, but she'd heard of them existing in the eastern US. "Do you have them in New York?

"Yeah, but not in the city."

Clyde rose up on his hind legs and stopped. Music carried lightly through the air. They were headed in the right direction. What party didn't have music? "That's where we're going, Clyde." She stepped next to him. He chittered, then ran as if he understood her.

They followed the music to a clearing filled with elfin teenagers. A partial silver moon hung in the sky surrounded by winking stars. Adjusted to the brightness and beauty of Aradia, Terra noted the air was wet and the temperature warm, reminding her of a rain forest.

"What are you waiting for?" Tania asked as she entered the field, Clyde beside her. He was more interested in the glowing creatures than the party.

The field flowed with music and elfin teens, mingling and dancing with drinks in their hands. None would take any notice of them, she hoped. Her short hair might be a giveaway. She thought of an excuse if anyone asked. Gum. Yeah. Her little brother put gum in it when she was sleeping. Did they have gum in Aradia? She would cross that bridge if she came to it.

Tania darted to the drink table decorated with rocks. Terra wasn't surprised. The girl was a rock-a-holic. She'd been so taken with the sparkling stones in Sier. They didn't quite glow like the flowers but shimmered in a rainbow of colors. She rejoined Terra with two cups in her hand. "I have moonbrew and a starbomb. I'm not sure what's in them," she said with a cheeky smile.

"Let's try both." The moonbrew was bitter and fizzy, similar to beer in Lols. Not her thing.

Tania's face contorted as she swallowed a sip of the starbomb. "Too sweet. Let's swap."

The sweet liquid drained down Terra's throat. It was the best thing she'd tasted since coming to Provence.

"Much better," Tania said after a swallow.

They mingled, sipped, and danced under the twinkling stars, fitting in like any other elves. Magic getting easier, she allowed the soft purring energy of the realm to flow through her, mixed with the starbomb. The stars vibrated and lights glowed across the field from the blue flowers. Voices amplified in her mind. Not a single voice but many.

She couldn't divert her eyes from the beauty until something, or someone, more beautiful walked in front of her – Tania. Her golden eyes the color of the moon over Sier. She'd loaned her an outfit for tonight, several over the past few days. They were roughly the same size. The colors looked good on her and the V neck of the blouse fit nicely over her chest. Terra's jeans a bit tight around Tania, displaying her rounded curves. Terra was a bit flatter in the trunk.

"Let's dance." Tania grabbed her hands and pulled, the smile on her face radiating. The starbomb flowing through her system, she let the music and Tania guide her movements. She hadn't been happier since she arrived in Provence than at the party, being a normal teenager with a knock-out like Tania by her side.

Their bodies moving closer as the music slowed down. Arms snaked around each other, their faces close enough the heat from Tania's breath warmed Terra's cheek. Their eyes met as their mouths moved closer. Terra's body bubbled with excitement as their lips touched.

"What are you doing here?" A male voice interrupted their tender moment.

They pulled apart from each other as if they were both guilty of a crime.

Kinzo stared at them with narrowed eyes. "Are you trying to get caught?" he said under his breath in irritation.

That was it. She wasn't invited and now this "friend" who didn't invite her was judging her. "I have to play elf, yet no elf accepts me as one!" She didn't care at all if anyone heard her or if she caused a scene.

"You weren't invited because no one wanted you to feel bad when you couldn't cross the curtain."

Oh really! Now she was enraged. Her not cross over a curtain. Nothing had impeded her yet! Terra blew out a large breath and grabbed Kinzo by the shoulders. "I'm here because I dropped the curtain!" She turned on her heel, walking away from him. He wasn't the kind of friend she needed.

"You see what you just did?" Tania said with disgust in her voice, walking away from Kinzo toward Terra.

Clyde immediately came to Terra's side and stood on his hind legs with his front paws lifted in his pick-me-up stance. "It was wrong wasn't it?" she asked, taking him in her arms. He climbed onto her shoulder, wrapping himself around her neck.

A warm hand entwined with hers. "Let's go," Tania suggested.

She had one friend and a good one. They shared secrets together. All the others, even though Meesha and Hyacinth and even Kayln were kind and acquaintances, they all shared a camaraderie with others like them. She had virtually no one like her except Tania, and well… now Cat.

Footfalls followed behind them as they entered the woods. "I'm sorry."

"Go away!" Tania snapped.

Kinzo jogged in front of them, his hair swaying. "Really, I'm sorry. We should have let you try. You did drop the curtain in Drakonia. What I don't understand is how you're here?" His gaze meeting Tania's.

She shrugged. "Do we need to figure this out now?"

That was about right. Who really cared to figure it out? The answer seemed simple. Tania was elfin too. She was more concerned with the flying glowy things. "Are these glowing, flying things pixies?"

Kinzo chuckled. "No, they are solaflies. You have a thing for pixies. What are they?" His eyebrows lowered into a V.

He was trying to be nice, change the topic. It wasn't working. She was too upset, not even angry just irritated, feeling slighted and dejected. "Nothing. Look, we're out of here. Go back to your party. I'm not wanted. I'm not like you. When Tania's gone, I'll be alone."

His eyes dropped in shame and Tania bumped his arm as they walked past him to rub in how awful he should feel. He could experience what it felt like to be slighted.

Tania adored how Terra did that. Change a subject as quickly as her mind flitted from one thought to the next. It had the effect of throwing a rock into a pond and scattering the water. In this case, the rock was confrontation with Kinzo and the scattering of the water was him laughing. Almost like he'd forgotten. Tania bet Terra hadn't.

She hadn't really liked Kinzo anyways. He seemed OK at first, but never visited once. It was like he wanted to forget he was a part of whatever rule they were breaking with her being there. All this stuff was foreign to her, but she was smart enough to figure out each was out for themselves, except Terra.

She'd visited every day, shared her food, clothes, and company. All the things true friends did. Guilt ate through Tania. How could she abandon Terra? At first, the adventure intrigued her, but after a week of hiding in a lycan home she wanted nothing more than to return to New York. To her life. The thought of leaving Terra to the two-faced crowd didn't sit right. "You're special. You can do things they can't."

"I know," Terra responded, her head hung and shoulders slumped. "Do you feel the energy here?"

"Kind of. It feels like everything is alive." She clutched the rock in her pocket that she'd taken from the table. The one she'd snuck out of Sier danced in her palm with a high energy pulse. The one from Aradia was softer, almost malleable. She wished she'd had more time to explore the other realms. The rocks were a souvenir of sorts, unlike anything she'd seen in her natural realm.

Terra lifted her head. "Yeah!" A smile returning to her oval face. The feature she loved the most was her eyes. They were three colors and changed. Something about her was more mystical than all the realms combined. As if she was a part of all of them and everything.

In the Shadows

When they reached the curtain, it dissolved as Terra walked through it and they were met with arguing. A tall, muscled young woman and a blonde prima princess-type were exchanging heated words that hung in the air as their eyes shifted to Terra and Tania.

18

Both Halsey and Meesha stared at Terra and Tania. Whatever they were arguing over, they stopped. The words dropping into oblivion.

"I knew it!" Meesha stated, folding her arms across her chest as if she knew some big secret. Obviously she recognized Tania as something different than elfin or fae, lycan, or whatever.

Even Meesha! That was the last straw. Terra was done. To heck with it all. They could banish her home for all she cared. "That I'm harboring a human. I am human. Oh, wait!" She threw her arms in the air. "You don't even call us human. No, that's been stripped from us too."

In the Shadows

Halsey squared her shoulders. "I told you she was up to something. She's why you're never in the room. Never have time for me," she said, directing her remarks at Tania and making the conversation about her.

Tania stepped forward, poking a finger into Halsey's chest. "And who are you that makes you more entitled than anyone else?"

Meesha didn't hide her chuckle. "That's what I was just saying. I'm Meesha, Terra's magic tutor."

"Tania, lost human."

Halsey pushed Tania's finger as if it was poison. "I'm the Diama of Navarin and she," Halsey pointed toward Terra, "is my roommate."

Terra stepped between them, her face inches from Halsey's, anger bubbling through every orifice. "You are a pathetic, entitled fae-wench. Every time you open your mouth and words come out they sound like metal twisting inward on itself!" The angry words flowed like molten steel. She didn't care if the fae-wench hated her and told all her fae friends.

Halsey's lips pouted and quivered. Tears welled in her blue eyes. She attempted to blink them away as they dropped onto her cheeks.

Terra stomped away. Patience for a spoiled fae was something Terra didn't have.

She'd been slighted by the elves, which burned like dry ice. Kinzo's sorry attempt to make amends enflamed her more and Meesha, who she thought was a friend, turned out to be as pathetic as everyone else. She didn't need a magic tutor anymore. She had it under control.

Tania rolled her eyes at the spoiled Diama and caught up to Terra. "She's horrid."

Horrid. That was a fitting word. "They all are! I'm going back with you. I'm not staying here any longer. I hate this place."

Crunching grass from footfalls made Terra turn her head. Meesha jogged toward them. "What more does she want?" she grumbled under her breath.

"You have every right to be upset. Please let me explain," she said with pleading eyes and body language.

Explain. Explain what exactly? That she followed her and waited. Why? What purpose did it serve? If Meesha wasn't six feet tall, she might consider decking her instead of folding her arms tight around her chest. "You stalked me."

"Not exactly. I went for a run in Canida and saw both of you leaving Sier. I'm a wolf. I have heightened senses, including sight and sound. I couldn't believe what I saw. That's why I came tonight. I wanted to see up close. I didn't know Halsey was there. She's the stalker," Meesha pleaded.

In the Shadows

Terra raked a hand through her hair. "You're right, sort of. I didn't tell anyone about her because they're looking for her. Telling you puts you in an awkward position." That was true, yet she was fine with telling Hyacinth only because she thought she could help. No, that wasn't even true. It did put them in a bad situation, but her and Tania had a hybrid thing.

Meesha's face was soft. "That's for me to decide. I can't imagine how weird it is for both of you here. Provence is sketchy to me and I've grown up with it."

"It's like living in a fish-bowl. You can see the outside world but can't touch it," Tania offered her thoughts out loud.

Terra always thought of it as a snow globe, but Tania's analogy was spot on too. The gist: they were trapped.

Meesha nodded. "How's your magic coming?"

Nice change of conversation, and Terra couldn't find it in herself to stay upset at Meesha. Heck, she was as curious as anyone. She might have done the same thing. They discussed it on their way back to the portable. Meesha left, but not without asking if she could help and making Terra promise to come to her if she could.

Terra lay back on the bed. No way was she going to her dorm tonight. The fae-wench could suffer a little. It might do her good. Besides, now that they'd entered Aradia they'd have another inking tonight.

Tania pulled the rock from her pocket. She'd clutched it tight in the heat of the moment when everything blew up. Ready to defend her friend who didn't need her help. Terra was capable. She gasped as she unfurled her hand. It was chartreuse, not a shimmery rainbow.

"What?" Terra asked, studying the stone. "Did you take that?"

Tania stumbled over her words, "It… it was… it was one of the rocks on the table. I don't understand what happened."

Terra had no clue either, but it had changed. "We aren't in Aradia anymore." Terra lifted her shoulders in a shrug, thinking maybe that was it and things from one realm changed when they entered others. It seemed plausible at least.

"I don't think so." Tania tugged a cabinet open and brought out a small crystal from Sier. She placed it on the table. "This one never changed."

She took souvenirs. Terra wasn't surprised; in fact, she was a bit envious because she hadn't thought of it. Terra visually inspected the rocks. "What was different this time?"

Tania laid her hands over Terra's. "I like you a lot and I was upset when they came at you. You don't need my help, but it angered me. Friends don't treat friends like that. We were having a good time, not bothering anyone, nobody knew I wasn't an elf. It was all good. Kinzo, then the blonde princess. I squeezed it in my palm, hard, and it heated in my hand for a second."

Off topic again, Terra barely heard what Tania said after 'I like you a lot'. "I like you a lot too. I've wanted to say something, but you're leaving and I…"

Tania smoothed the back of her hand over Tania's cheek. "We have tonight."

"This could be our last chance," Terra said as their lips met. Warmth traveled over Terra as they kissed and galaxies collided.

19

Hyacinth flipped her dark, sleek hair behind her as she walked through the curtain. She didn't have to touch it like Terra did. Terra thought of the marks on her chest. Last night, after Aradia, as they slept, a tree began to form on each of their chests. Other than Tania, she hadn't shown anyone, nor asked if they had them too. Maybe they were like a key or something and allowed easy passage into realms.

They'd decided rock changing was Tania's magic. It was possible hybrid powers worked differently. Her mind drifted back to last night. They'd curled on the bed as they had after Sier. Clyde between them, his breath under the covers diminishing the pain from the inking of the new marks. Tania held her hand. 'I wish you could come with me, but you can't. Not because someone will notice, but you have incredible power. I can feel it.'

Hyacinth's brother, Devan, interrupted Terra's thoughts. "They just took the guards away. We should be safe, but I think we need to go a little farther in. We don't want anyone coming through the curtain as I'm portalling. The diplomats travel on Sundays," he explained.

He was a year or two older than Hyacinth, with short, sun-kissed blonde hair, green eyes, twin dimples, and an adorable Australian accent. Vampires, unable to have children of their own, adopted. It made her wonder about the normal life span of a vampire. They were immortal, but could also die again under the right circumstances.

Sandy rock and the ruby red sky made Drakonia a depressing, horrible place to visit. There was no plant life or animals, as far as she could tell. It was a wasteland with a blood river that weaved its way through it. She couldn't understand how anyone would ever want to visit. Even Provence, the snow globe, was better. The blood stench that made her gag the first time she visited didn't bother her as much this time. By the cringe on Tania's face, she smelled it, or being in Drakonia brought back memories of being drenched in the blood of dead humans. Terra squeezed her hand gently for comfort.

The last time she was here she remembered cities on the horizon. From the distance they looked tiny, but to see them from where she stood the buildings must be skyscrapers filled with glass due to their reflection. She'd also taken note of the invisible curtain. It too had a symbol etched into it like the others. She simply hadn't noticed the first time. The group followed Devan around the rocks to an area not visible to anyone entering or exiting the curtain.

"This will do," he said, coming to a stop. The bland, tan, smooth rocks carved into an overhang.

This was it. Terra wanted to leave, go with her, but Tania was right: she had to stay. It wasn't her powers, which she was only just learning she possessed, but something inside. She couldn't put a finger on it. Leaving wasn't an option. There was something she felt she needed to do.

Facing Tania, dark hair settled in waves on one side of her face, her nose ring shining with the reddish glow of the sky. She was beautiful. Terra took her hands. "I hate goodbyes."

Tania pulled her into a hug, her arms feeling everything right around her. She then pulled away a couple inches and gently pressed her hands to Terra's face. "It's not goodbye." Her golden-brown eyes meeting Terra's.

Their lips met and pressed in a kiss. A spinning teal vortex opened behind Tania, but Terra barely noticed. Tania pulled away. Terra reached for her hands as she stepped backwards toward the vortex.

Air sizzled and cracked around them like lightning. Matter moved from two seams in the atmosphere. One a couple feet from her and Tania, the other behind Hyacinth and Devan. Four vampires, two from each split, appeared. She assumed those were portals. Her mind blown, she was speechless, shocked. How did they know?

"Close the portal," a tall man with short, dark hair demanded.

Terra swallowed. This was it. They'd been caught. She didn't care about herself, but Tania had to go home. Without time to think about her actions she pushed Tania towards the vortex, hoping to get her through before it closed. Tania reached for her hand and fell backwards onto the smooth rock as the portal vanished.

"I'm so sorry." Terra rushed to her friend, dropping by her side. "I thought I could—.

"I know." She reached out and cupped her hands over Terra's.

"Are you done here?" a vampire woman asked in an irritated tone, her eyebrows lowered and face crunched in annoyance.

No, she wasn't! Terra tilted her head upwards and took in the person attached to the voice. A vampire. Her light hair pulled so tight in a ponytail she saw her veins throbbing under her skin. Which struck her odd. Did vampires have a beating heart and veins?

The vampire's eyes were unusually tiny and her face long with low cheek bones. "Get up!" she ordered.

Terra stood. She wasn't about to be intimidated by a vampire; an ugly vampire in an even uglier red leather costume. She squared her shoulders, ready to face off if need be. "Who are you to tell us what to do?"

The woman's small, round eyes narrowed more. Ignoring Terra's question she pushed her to the side, forcing Terra to stumble from her strength. She then motioned for Tania – who was now standing – to turn around and wrapped something metallic around her wrists, banding them together. Terra wanted to take a swing at the woman. How dare she?

"What are you doing? She needs to get home!" Terra demanded. "Let her go."

The tall man with short, dark hair spoke, "She doesn't belong here or in Lols. She's a lost soul. Given her age, she might have been provided a second chance, maybe she still will if she cooperates."

In the Shadows

A lost soul? She wasn't just a soul but had a physical form too. A second chance? What was he talking about? She stamped her foot in frustration then glanced to Hyacinth and Devan, pleading with her eyes for help. Hyacinth shot her an 'I'm sorry' glance. The other two vampires stood behind them. There was no help.

The dark-haired male vamp strolled in front of Hyacinth. "We'll forget about this for now. I'm sure there's something we'll need in the future. Take the elf and return to school." He rotated on his heel, addressing Devan, "You're coming with us."

"No," Terra grumbled as the female vamp grabbed her wrists behind her back and forced her forward. Stumbling and fighting each step, she glanced over her shoulder as she was dragged away from Tania.

Another teal vortex appeared, and Tania was pushed through it. Not with ease but with force, her eyes meeting Terra's for a second before she vanished with the other vampires.

She and Hyacinth were pushed through another portal. The energy inside her brimming for a moment. She reached her hand out to touch it, as if she could mold it, then it vanished.

Terra and Hyacinth landed awkwardly behind Provence Academy. Terra glanced at her friend. She'd done it. Their friendship was over. Her brother was in trouble and they would be soon too. She didn't believe for a second they'd got off. Even if they did, knowing the vampires had Tania was worse. "I'm so sorry," Terra pleaded to Hyacinth.

Hyacinth stood and dusted herself off, giving Terra a hand. "That was a rough landing. Devan will be fine. He's a master manipulator in sticky situations. Trust me. Tania is the one you should worry about."

She already was. The words stuck in Terra's throat longer than normal. "Are they going to turn her over to the harvesters?" She cringed at the thought. That was worse, as they'd extract her soul and spill her blood, contributing to Blood River.

"No. I doubt it. If that was the case, it would have been done properly. This was a covert operation. Someone is interested in her and the only person with that much clout in Drakonia is Minister M'ra. She's a human who evaded capture. She slipped through harvesting, fell into Blood River, then hid for several days. That's not a thing that happens, ever. For now, she's safe, but their questioning tactics can be brutish. We need a plan."

20

Metford and Bane

Metford fixed his eyes on the debonair vampire. His charm and expensive attire couldn't help him now. The plan was to turn the girl over. The vampires reneged on the deal. She was their soul. "Where is the girl?!" demanded Metford. His eyes black with anger.

Bane brushed a finger over his nail. "She'll be returned. We have a few questions for her first."

"You don't have that privilege. She's ours and must be returned within 48 hours or any deal we had is off the table. Her soul will go to the Otherworld. End of story." The original deal, had her harvesting gone correctly, was to send her to Tranquility or hand her over to the vampires for a second chance. That deal was off the table now. When they got her back he would do everything in his power to give her a second chance at life. Not as a vampire, but to return her to Lols.

In the past, in the nearly twenty years since Cyrus's disappearance, vampires had collected only teenagers. Not once had they any request for someone older. Metford understood it was their relentless pursuit of Cyrus. He wouldn't be hiding in a teenager's body, but maybe he'd fathered a child. That's what he assumed the vampires were searching for. Lost spawn. It was a baseless witch hunt.

Bane, who never prickled a hair over someone's discomfort, raised his eyes from the fingernail he brushed and stared at something on the wall that Metford couldn't see through the holocall. "No need for all that. She will be returned, alive." Forty-eight hours, he couldn't promise. It was M'ra herself that ordered the girl taken. The questioning tactics would be rough, but the girl wouldn't be killed.

"One more thing." Metford tugged at his beard. "We've brought everyone home from the Otherworld. They will not be going back, not for your witch hunt." He was usually mild-mannered and diplomatic, but this was over the top. The girl was theirs. Yes, they'd return her alive, but she'd never be the same.

Terra was glad she hadn't taken Clyde. Who knows what they may have done to a harmless ferret. Meesha opened her door after Terra knocked.

Meesha's eyes searched Terra's. "What happened?" Terra had a hard time hiding emotions, and the lycan picked up on her sadness immediately.

Terra wrapped her arms around the lycan's solid middle and wept. She couldn't halt the tears from running down her face. First her father, then moving to Provence, and now her friend. Someone she had very real and deep feelings for was taken.

Meesha folded Terra in her arms. "Hey, Clyde needs some outdoor time. Why don't we go for a walk? You can tell me everything."

Terra let go and sucked up her sniffles, accepting a few tissues from Meesha's troll roommate's tail plumage. "Thank you."

The troll nodded. Her tail a bright canary yellow, her face friendly and sweet, with her round cheeks and big, lavender eyes.

Clyde climbed the banister and slid down as they took one step at a time. He chased his tail in circles as he waited. He was more than ready to have outdoor time. Terra chuckled at his silly behavior. Almost always, he found a way to make her laugh. She didn't bother with the harness.

"Why the tears?" Meesha asked as she pushed the huge double doors open.

"They took her. The vampires." She relayed the whole story and every detail as they were still fresh in her mind.

Meesha sat on the grass beneath a tree with silvery-lavender leaves. "What do the vampires want with her? I thought the harvesters wanted her. She was, you know…" Meesha couldn't say the words.

No one could really say the words. They were hard enough to think without actually forming them and spitting them out. "I don't know, but Hyacinth says we need a plan. I came to get Clyde, but that's not all. I need to reach more magic."

Meesha leaned back on her elbows. "Magic comes in many forms. The best defense is a good offense. I think it's time for your next lesson."

Terra listened to Meesha as she watched Clyde bounce and scamper. Lesson two was the prey species. The fae used a three-pronged approach; land, sea, and air. The sea fae, or water fae, had venom in their scales which makes anything that takes a bite out of them sick. The air fae used their colorful plumage and feathers to confuse predators. They also spit salt-water, as do the sea fae. The land fae shift into unicorns. Their power is in their horn. They have the ability to create portals and send their attackers into oblivion, turn people into stone or ash, and the most powerful can temporarily turn someone into something else, such as a harmless bug. All fae design spells, and use, make, and develop potions of all kinds.

"OK, so you're telling me someone like Halsey can turn me into an ant?"

"Yup, but I don't think she's that powerful, at least not yet. Being the Diama doesn't give her more power, it just makes her more popular and sets the weight of one-day running Navarin on her shoulders." Meesha's voice had a compassionate ring to it as if she felt sorry for her.

Nope! Never. Terra didn't like her one bit. The fae-wench stalked her, looked down on her, and treated her like nothing more than a peasant. "Don't do that. She's a fae-wench."

Meesha nodded. "She is, but that brattiness isn't something she was born with. It was learned from her parents and fae society. Could you imagine knowing your entire life you have no choice but to run the realm?"

Terra didn't want to hear it. Halsey was the worst person she'd ever met, but Meesha sowed the seed and now parts of her shield were cracking and traces of forgiveness were coming through. That was enough about the fae-wench. "What about elves or trolls?"

"Two more things about the fae; they are well-read, so are the elves, and they have a weakness – iron." She sighed and leaned forward, crossing her legs.

Iron. Terra would need to remember that. It could be a great fae-wench repellent.

Meesha continued as Clyde chased his tail between them. "The elves. First rule: never underestimate them. They weave and sew fabrics from the plants in their realm. They also communicate telepathically with other species in the realm; not just the plants, but other elves, bugs, animals. I'm pretty sure they communicate with the dirt too. They are also healers, but can be ruthless. The ancient texts, which you can thank them for paper, describe how everything in the realm attacks during war. Vines appear from nowhere, roots pull soldiers under, and little flying bugs dig under a dragon's tough skin, making them itch. It's a kamikaze mission. They do have a weakness though: they are allergic to dreadwood which grows like a weed in some realms. It makes them crazy."

In Aradia she'd felt the energy. It was alive, as Meesha described. Terra wasn't sure about being elfin anymore though. She had none of the skills except good reading comprehension. She'd always scored grade levels ahead. She made a mental note to find out more about dreadwood. Were hybrid elves allergic to it?

Clyde scampered away, then formed a ball and rolled between them.

"Trolls are miners. Verboten is filled with gems and precious metals. They make swords, jewelry, the crown Halsey will wear one day. They are clever and like to bargain. In times of war they have the coolest defenses. Those plumes on their tails are part of their camouflage. They roll into balls with their plumage showing. They look like nothing more than these odd birds in the realm called folibees."

Terra chuckled, envisioning a troll rolled into a ball. She couldn't imagine how they contorted their bodies in that way. It hurt her to do a back bend. Meesha continued, explaining how they also dreamwalk and can distort their surroundings to make themselves invisible, blending into any environment. Their weakness is salt water. It melts their skin off.

"Ew. That's gross."

Meesha raised a corner of her lip. "right."

"What about harvesters?"

"We'll talk about them in lesson three. They are neither predator nor prey." Meesha shook out her arms. "Today I want you to tune into your elfin magic. Listen and speak to the plants."

That was easy in Aradia, but she hadn't tried it since, nor had she had a conversation at any point with a plant. They'd merely pointed her and Tania in the right direction. She let out a deep breath and closed her eyes. It always helped her concentrate better.

She easily found the water trickling beneath them. She wasn't sure anymore if that was a predator trait or prey. If the elves did communicate with other things, maybe she was tuning in to life in the stream. As she did in Aradia, she asked a question from her mind, sending it out. *Can you place a beautiful silver-lavender leaf on my head?*

She opened her eyes as something brushed against her hair and felt the top of her head. A leaf. She'd done it!

Meesha laughed. "A leaf, clever. It worked."

Terra was ready to go again. In the portal, she felt as if she could bend it to her will. There was something she picked up from the portal. Its energy. All energy, she was learning, had a signature, but inside the portal, for that short moment that probably didn't last but half a second, she felt its movement like jelly. If only she could find a way to mold it.

In the Shadows

Her eyes closed, she didn't focus on the water or the plants, but the energy surrounding her until a map similar to what she'd seen in Sier appeared in her mind. Vertical and horizontal lines similar to latitude and longitude circled Provence City. The image and lines weren't clear, like looking at them through cloudy water. Provence was a tiny ball surrounded by more lines that spanned into the other realms with no apparent end. She popped her eyes open. "You won't believe me!"

21

Tania

The plum paint wasn't Tania's taste, but no one was sucking her blood. They hadn't even showed fang. She was more than a little nervous being stuck in a realm with vampires who might eat her for a snack. As a nervous habit, she ran her fingers along the velvet armrest of the couch.

"You avoided capture for a week. That's a record. Most never make it out of Drakonia or Thraves. Tell me, how did you do it?" the tall, dark-skinned vampire asked, her back to Tania as she ran a finger along the stone fireplace.

She certainly wasn't telling her where she hid, or anything about her stay. Terra was her priority and her helpful vamp friends, not this woman in her tight, black pin-skirt and turquoise blouse. "I landed in the river and was covered in blood." She shuddered at the memory. "From there I couldn't see anything because blood kept dripping in my eyes and it stung. I ended up in that weird little town and found a geyser, then a cave. That's where I hid."

The woman turned around. "How exactly did you get from Drakonia to Provence?"

Tania shrugged. "I walked."

The woman pinched her heavily painted pink lips. "You walked." She sauntered closer. "Walked. The curtain shouldn't open for you or your elf friend."

Tania tried to hide her visible tremble at the vampire's emphasis on 'elf friend'. "You think I wanted to fall through a cave, land in a large puddle of blood, then spend a week in a town filled with freaks?"

"Probably not." She stood in front of Tania, staring down at her through almond-shaped eyes. "Where else have you been?"

Tania pinched the velvet with her fingers to maintain some composure as she pretended to act like she had no idea what the vamp was talking about. "Nowhere. There was nowhere to go."

The vampire brought a long, pointed fingernail to Tania's neck. Her pulse raced and she hoped the vampire didn't sense it as they always did in the movies. Then she dragged her nail from the tip of her shirt downward, making a clean cut. "Those marks say different."

The tattoos, or marks were, exposed. She tried the Terra distraction thing. "You just ripped my friend's shirt!"

Unconvinced by the act, and not the least distracted, the vampire didn't take her eyes off Tania's.

This vampire was harsh and smart. She hadn't done it right. It always worked for Terra, but her mind always seemed to flit from thought to thought like a butterfly. "Fine. I met Terra as she was walking her ferret and she took me to Aradia because she's elfin. The other one I wandered into by accident." The story sounded believable, but was she convincing?

The vampire stepped away and sat on the other end of the couch. "Tell me about your life before you fell through a cave," she said, waving a hand.

"I'm a student at NYU, still undecided on my major but currently working on a bachelor's in geology. I know it's really general, but it gets me all the science credits I need if I switch to something else—"

The vampire interrupted her mid-sentence. "Not what I can read in your file," she said, visibly frustrated. "Did you have any magic? Any special skills?"

Magic? File? Did they have a file on everyone that was harvested? Tania hadn't known magic was real until a week ago. Sure, there were witches on Earth. Was she still on Earth? She was distracting herself with Terra's distraction tactic. Why didn't it work on the vamp? "I can do this," she said, then stuck her hand under her armpit and made it fart.

The vampire's pink lips tightened and her almond eyes narrowed. "I've been nice. There are other ways of getting information from you that don't require your cooperation." Tania was sure that had something to do with sucking her blood.

The vampire's expression suddenly softened as she changed tactics. "As vampires we have unlimited access to Lols. We can bring you anything you want to eat."

Food was the way to her heart right now. The fruits Terra brought were good and she shared her stash of beef jerky, but it wasn't enough to fill her up. "A big plate of spaghetti, thick meatballs, and garlic bread from Flavio's in New York."

"I can make it happen."

What she wouldn't do for food. But she wasn't the kind of person to betray someone's trust. The vampire was looking for something. Some magical skill. Tania had no magic except molding the rock from Aradia.

The stones were in her pocket and no way was she sharing that with the vampire. "I'm a pretty boring, normal human. I'm not sure what you're looking for. Can you give me a hint?"

"You like science; rocks and caves. Why do they interest you?"

"It's not just the rocks and caves, but finding hidden worlds buried beneath the surface of Earth."

The vampire stood, pressed her hands along her skirt, and walked to the door. The handle in her grip, she said, "When I return, I will have your dinner."

22

The Tribunal

Maglesh stood. As the first order of business, he took priority. The elf girl could wait. She wasn't nearly as important as what he had to share. "The veil is weakening more each day and some subspecies are taking advantage. A dragon was seen over Verboten the evening of Day 5. I have the footage." He rested his eyes on the five dragons.

With a tap from his tail, he touched the comicay. Its image displayed for all thirty-five diplomats to see. A brown dragon soared over the land. Its wings spread wide.

"Nonsense!" roared Colton as he stood. His large form dwarfed any troll and his red hair appeared as flames on his head. He was the second dragon, and a fire-dragon with a fiery attitude to match. "Not a single dragon would fly over your realm!"

Rosette cleared her throat. She wasn't one to meddle in dragon business, but they'd all seen the footage. "Then how do we explain what we saw?"

"It wasn't us!" Colton said, his voice rumbling the building, then took his seat.

"The problem is the veil. It's weakening and something needs to be done to ensure the safety of all," replied Maglesh who hadn't shown the comicay footage to start a war with dragons. That was the last thing he wanted. No, he wanted the dramatic effect to wake everyone up from their complacent attitude. The veils had separated their realms since ancient times. He shuddered to think of the battles that ensued before the veils.

Olivia rose from her seat. She was a junior fae and sat at seat five. She nearly always kept her mouth shut, but this was something she had a solution for even if only a temporary one. It might work until something more permanent could be arranged. "My family designed a potion that mended the veils in Navarin. We don't know for how long." She sat, slicking her skirt beneath her as she did so.

"Why haven't you brought this to the tribunal sooner?" asked Maglesh.

She stood again. "Well, we don't know how permanent it is. It's a test. We've tried other things in the past that worked at first but didn't last. This time it's been months."

The eldest fae, Liam, turned his head to offer her his appreciation. It meant a lot to Olivia.

"Does this potion require a heart?" Lukas, the eldest lycan, asked.

Olivia smiled meekly. She was young but understood his reference. The great Merla was her ancestor, and they still used her potions and spells but it wasn't any potion or spell he was referencing. "No, but it does need something that is found in every realm — limestone and hemlock."

The book was where Cat told Terra it would be. She'd always wanted to climb a big library ladder and roll. It hadn't been as fun or as interesting as she'd imagined.

Terra scanned through the pages searching for the section on hybrids. The text was ancient, with thick parchment paper, and some was written in code or a language she couldn't understand. Mid-way through she found what she was searching for.

Hybrids had always existed under the cloak of the realm they belonged to the most.

Their magic manifested in ways unseen to purebloods. That explained Cat becoming a catfish. The combination gave them unique skill sets. In ancient days, wars started over discovered hybrids as they were sentenced to the Land of Lost Souls. Families were ripped apart, children taken from their parents. Sometimes an entire family was banished to Lols, other times they left by their own choice.

Terra was disgusted at such barbaric behavior. It was no wonder her parents left. It sickened her more that, in modern times, some still believed in the old ways. Taking a child from their family was no answer. She turned the page to a detailed drawing of a young girl. Her long hair flowed in the wind. She was the most famous of hybrids. Her name: Amber.

Amber was a fae-elf-troll-lycan hybrid with strong magical abilities. She could shift herself and others, shoot magic beams from her hands, put up a shield and manipulate the mind to see what wasn't there. She was to be destroyed and her family sent to Lols until a sea fae – Merla – stood in front of all the realms and offered a solution – to put veils between them.

The words beneath were smudged and Terra was unable to read them. Sitting back in the plush chair, she sorted through what she'd read. The realms had been open at one time.

Anyone could travel from one to another. It was fear and savagery that changed everything. And Amber, a mix of four, like Terra. She'd been to Drakonia, Sier, Canida, and Aradia. Did she, too, have magic as strong as Amber?

No. It wasn't magic inside her but her ability to manipulate magic. Meesha taught her that on her first lesson. It boggled her mind all the things she may be able to do. The lines and maps were unique. She just didn't understand yet what to do with them.

She put the book back, but on the return cart, and stepped outside with Clyde riding in her backpack. At breakfast, the whole group decided they were in. She'd even forgiven Kinzo. Not that her anger toward him lasted more than that night. By the next day she was over it. Hyacinth insisted they meet before dinner at the portable. No one would look for them there and, with the curtains always drawn, no one would see them should anyone pass.

When she entered, everyone was already present and seated at the table; Kinzo and Nalysse, Kayln, Meesha, Caspen, and Hyacinth. Happy tears bubbled in the corners of her eyes. They all made the choice and she was overwhelmed.

They'd pulled up chairs and set them around the table. There was one more for Terra. She joined them.

Hyacinth got right to business. "We all have abilities and we're going to need them. Terra and I are the only ones that can enter Drakonia. I'm not sure how." She glanced at Terra.

"I may know," Terra offered, ready to share what she'd learned about hybrids and her marks. "I was in the library. There was an ancient hybrid who had awesome magic. It works different for hybrids." She continued telling them about Amber. "Tania is a hybrid like me. All commoners are. She went into Drakonia, Sier, and Aradia with me."

All eyes on Terra, she had their attention. "There's something else." She pulled her shirt down, displaying her markings. A dragon at the 12:00 position, an infinity symbol at the 8:00, a tree at the 3:00, and a wolf at the 1:00.

The silent words passed between them until Kayln spoke. "You've been to four realms! Five, if you include Lols, but everyone can go there just nobody wants to which is why nobody cares they don't know how to get there - except vampires." Her words rambled and she shut up as nasty looks were tossed her way.

Hyacinth turned her eyes toward Kayln, not because of her insensitive comment about vampires but to visually say 'shut up'. "This is serious."

Kayln did. Terra was thankful. All her rambling was disturbing. At this point, she knew her well enough she didn't take it personal. Fae were smug.

"You're saying hybrids can come and go. They get passports for each realm?" Nalysse asked, a tinge of jealousy in her tone.

Is that what they call them — passports? Terra thought.

Caspen, whose dark hair seemed curlier tonight, answered the question. "It makes sense. Since ancient times they've been banishing hybrids to Lols. Over time, those hybrids had hybrid children. When some passed they became vampires."

"That's why I adore you," Hyacinth said, giving him a kiss on the cheek. She then turned her focus to the group. "This is more serious than I think you realize. I have friends in the realm and they've taken her to the Tower." She scanned their faces. "Minister M'ra's Tower."

Terra didn't know a thing about Minister M'ra but the look on Hyacinth's face and the warning in her words said everything she needed to know.

Kinzo pulled his arms onto the table and folded his hands together. "We need to learn everything we can about Tania. What makes her so special the head vampire has her? What does she want from her? We have the library. There're a lot of ancient texts, we have ears to listen. We need to spend more time in town overhearing adult conversations. Meesha, Hyacinth, turn your predator ears on."

Terra turned to Hyacinth. "How long do you think we have?"

"It's hard to say. My guess is the tribunal doesn't know about Tania or the situation. Harvesters and vampires have a love/hate relationship. Our realms touch and so we have to get along, but sometimes we may double cross the other," Hyacinth said with a wince of disapproval.

"No comicays, either when you're doing or speaking anything you want to keep secret," Terra added. She believed they tracked better than GPS and had suspicions others, such as parents and the council, maybe even realm leaders, could access memories through them.

Hyacinth covered her nose and mouth with both hands. Terra admired the deep blue polish on her nails. "That's how they knew." She turned to Terra. "I'm so sorry. I'm so used to it I never take it off." She dropped her hands, her tone angry as understanding stung in the brain. "They use them to spy on us!"

Judging by their faces, most of them had never considered it. It would have shocked her, but these kids were different. More innocent, in a sense, than humans. Her friends at home knew parents track their GPS.

In this case, comicays had the added invasion of accessing memories, which made them far more dangerous. She couldn't be upset. Hyacinth didn't turn them in on purpose, but this did prove her hypothesis about comicays.

"No more comicays. We can't change the past. Let's divvy up what needs to be done," Nalysse suggested.

23

Terra hadn't gone to the dorm after Tania'd been taken. Her empty heart couldn't take the loneliness nor could she handle the fae-wench. She'd spent the night in the portable, curled on the bed thinking about Tania. But she couldn't stay gone forever. At some point she had to face Halsey.

There was no time like the present, she thought as she pushed the door open. Halsey sat on her bed in a baby blue nightgown, a leg tucked beneath her as she brushed her silky blonde hair. She set the brush on the table beside her bed and lay down, her back facing Terra's bed.

Terra hated to do this but it was the right thing and Meesha's guilt trip worked on her. "I'm sorry. I said mean things."

Halsey turned over. "You aren't sorry. You meant them. Everybody else likes me. I don't know why you don't." She rolled her eyes.

Of course she meant them, but that didn't mean she couldn't apologize for them now. What was it with the fae-wench? "I did mean them. You're spoiled and you don't have any friends. Your subjects don't count. They have to like you or pretend they do."

Halsey's eyes teared up. She wasn't even trying to be mean. She was being Terra. Brutally honest. "Listen, I know that was mean too, but it's true, and those tears are because you know it's true." She paused, relenting to her forgiving side. Holding grudges was never a good idea. "I haven't really given you a chance either."

Halsey sucked up her tears. "No, you haven't."

Trust was something earned and Halsey hadn't, but she could give her a chance. A small one, tiny even. "Let's get to know each other." She pulled her phone out of her drawer and brought up her pictures then sat beside Halsey. "This is my home."

Halsey was taken with the phone and the pictures. She asked questions about her dad, her mom. She even acknowledged that maybe she was homesick. That was the most empathy she'd shown and at least demonstrated it was possible for her. For the first time since she'd met her, Halsey laughed. It wasn't the pigeon laugh Terra expected, but more of a giggle followed by a short snort.

When it was Halsey's turn, she showed memories from her comicay. A series of islands covered in seafoam green sand in the Lavender Seas. Bioluminescent algae-like plants made the seas shine at night. Now the sparkly lavender paint made a lot of sense. It really was beautiful in a mythical sort of way.

Terra had another question, a fae question. It might not tell her much, but she was curious. "What can you tell me about Merla, the great sea-fae?"

24

Tania

Tania stretched as she opened her eyes. Her body snuggled onto the velvet couch. Not a single window in the room, she had no idea how long she'd been out and she remembered nothing after wolfing down the spaghetti and meatballs. Was it the carb load that put her to sleep?

Pulling the rocks out of her pocket, she squished them into her palms and let go, revealing the rocks hadn't changed. She put them together and squeezed. When she opened her palm they looked the same. She meshed them over and over but nothing happened. Maybe it was coincidence that she changed the Aradian rock.

When the doorknob rattled she tucked the rocks back into her pockets. Dismayed to see the same female vamp with two other vamps. She'd come to think of her as Queen Akasha from Queen of the Damned. She looked a lot like her but with shimmering pink lipstick.

This visit, she wore a fuchsia-colored lady suit. The two extra vamps hung by the door as if she'd try and escape or something. Like she could actually outrun them. They stood quietly, one on each side of the door like secret service. The female in a dark blue pant suit with her hair coiled in a tight bun and the male in a black suit, his dark hair slicked and short.

Tania explored the idea that maybe in her human life Queen Akasha had been an FBI or DEA agent. She hadn't seen her in anything but suits. She had the attitude as well. She didn't have to get angry to get under Tania's skin and make her nervous.

"Tell me about the rocks you polished when you were 10?"

What kind of a question was that? They were everyday rocks, not anything special and weathering and water polished rocks. "How do you know about that…?" Her words hung in the air as she realized they'd invaded her mind. That's the only way anyone could know that. She hadn't even told her parents.

An even worse thought entered her head. They fed her drugged food. That's why they were so nice and gave her exactly what she asked for. She stomped herself mentally and blamed it on food deprivation.

The vamp sat on the plush chair to the side of Tania, her legs slightly together and to the side while she waited. It was the patience that drove Tania nuts. It wasn't that the vamps had patience, they just acted as though they did. That's why they intruded in her mind. The more she thought about it the angrier she grew. "Since you were in my mind you would know that after the event I came down with pneumonia. Those rocks I thought I polished with my mind were probably an illusion. I was in bed for weeks."

"Hmm," the vampire sighed. "It seems we have one more test. Bill and Sally will escort you."

The vampire secret service had names, and really ordinary ones at that. Once she was over the plain Jane names she grew angrier, heat rising in her cheeks. They'd traipsed through her memories, what other torture could they possibly do that was worse? The two vamps by the door moved to Tania's side and lifted her off the couch. Neither said a word as they forcibly escorted her out of the room. She could walk on her own. This was a show of brute force, that was it. They were stronger than her and wanted to make sure she kept to her place. She took in the creamy hallway, modern-style tea light sconces, and a stone floor. With the absence of windows everything was lit by light bulbs in matching stylish holders.

They entered another room only feet away from the one she was in. It wasn't as welcoming, with its white walls and sterile appearance. There was a single blue chair, something like the kind she sat in at the dentist office and a tray of tools beside it. This was worse! They saved the horror for last. "No!" she yelled as she tried to free herself from their grasp.

Her weak kicking and punching was futile against their strength. They didn't even flinch as they stuffed her into the chair. She fought it with all her human might but she was no match for them. Metal clips fastened over her ankles, wrists, waist, and legs. She literally couldn't move. "What are you doing?"

The lady vamp returned and stood in front of Tania as Sally and Bill poked needles into her arms, neck, and thighs. "When commoners refuse to cooperate, we have other methods."

They were going to siphon her blood. "You have no right! It's mine, belongs to me. You have an entire river and falls filled with blood!"

Her protests didn't even get an eye roll or glance. So far, the vamp experience had been mildly unpleasant and it bothered her they went into her mind without her permission, but taking her blood was too much. "It's illegal to take someone's blood without permission," she persisted.

The Queen Akasha vamp laughed; a solid, evil cackle. "We are vampires. Blood is what we do. Don't worry, we only need five shots. I brought in our best tasters, but the blood must be fresh so we can do it this way or I'll have them take it straight from you."

Tania's eyes widened and her pulse quickened. If this was the easy way, she was better off taking it. The idea of someone biting through her flesh to suck her blood made her neck veins sting in phantom protest. She tried to calm herself in fear her blood would siphon too quick with her heartbeat elevated. *Breathe, breathe, think of your happy place.*

Bill and Sally pulled the needles and tubes from her arms. *That was it?* She was all worked up over that? One glance at the lady vamp and she knew better than to complain. She imagined she'd be happy to put the needles back in and drink, using the thin tubes as a straw, or worse...

All three left without another word and she was still strapped to the chair. She felt violated, but was eased that it wasn't painful and didn't last longer than seconds.

The metal cuffs around her wrists, ankles, waist, and legs clicked and opened. She glanced around the room to see who was there. No one. She was alone. Then a lock clicked and the door slid open a crack.

25

Metford and Bane

Metford beeped on the comicay, his face popping into Bane's head. The forty-eight hours was up. He wanted the girl. Would demand her, but the latest development wouldn't please him. Somehow they'd lost her again. She was slippery for a commoner. Luckily, her blood samples gave them something else. Something that would put the harvester in order and keep their little secret.

Bane depressed the comicay and Metford appeared in the middle of the room, his expression a mixture of aggravation and anger as he tugged harder at his chestnut goatee than usual.

"Your time is past up. Where is she?" he demanded.

Yup! Anger and aggravation. He could explain this and give him a little something to keep him quiet. "There's been a complication." It was a bit more than a complication. She'd been strapped to a chair with metal cuffs in a room with no windows and a 6-inch-thick metal door that opened by eye scan. How she got away was a mystery. Not that Metford needed all the details, just the pertinent ones.

The harvester's eyes beamed black again, forcing Bane to look away. The black was worse than the swirling color.

He flipped his top as he yelled. "You lost her, again!" Metford's voice radiating disappointment. How could they? He was furious and didn't hide it.

It was best he didn't mention how she escaped. They'd violated tribunal covenants and M'ra had no more use for her. Her blood showed she wasn't who they wanted. It had shown other fascinating facts. "Yes, she escaped." He twirled his chair to the side to avoid the stare he felt burning into him from the harvester. "Her blood showed something very interesting. She is an elf-troll-lycan-dragon and harvester hybrid." He played his card.

In the Shadows

"That's not possible," Metford said in shock. Harvesters didn't mingle with the other realms. When they harvested, they did so in their spirit form. It allowed them to see souls. They didn't visit Lols in their physical form, no one did. Not a single harvester had been banished to Lols in centuries.

All commoners were hybrids, but none were harvester hybrids. It was a once in a millennia event. "It doesn't happen often, I'll give you that. But she can enter five realms, six when you include Drakonia." That wasn't the piece that astounded Metford but it was interesting.

Metford insisted, his voice relaying his distrust, "You're sure she is harvester?"

About what Bane expected, but he could prove it. "Very much. The minister used our best tasters. They don't make mistakes, and all five agreed she is harvester." Each taster was in a different room when a shot of her blood was taken directly from the source and provided to them. They all had the same analysis. "I'd be happy to share a sample for you to test."

Metford's face twisted in agony, as if he was the one losing blood. "Yes. I'll need that." He wasn't planning on testing it, nor was he planning on giving the chief the sample. That would spark a DNA matching investigation, including all harvesters young and old, to trace blood lines.

REALM WALKER

Halsey was a wealth of fae information and offered much on Merla's story, which was gory in Terra's opinion. There was infighting between the realms often sparked by hybrids, as the book suggested, but that wasn't all. Often, petty things sparked skirmishes between the realms. Lives were lost. Merla hated the violence. She was a powerful water fae who lived in a cave beneath the Lavender Seas. In order to put a stop to their hate and prejudice, she came up with a powerful spell that was as harsh as the wars. She demanded the hybrid, Amber, be brought to her along with the attention of every realm.

A spell to divide the realms and stop the fighting required a sacrifice from each realm. She needed an elf, a harvester, a vampire, a lycan, a dragon, and a land fae. Halsey said it was the horn she needed because of its magical powers. It was after that land fae became the dominant, royal fae. Terra was pretty sure that was to save Merla's kind, the water fae, but hadn't said it.

She also demanded six hybrids, one from each realm. Once the demands were met she took Amber home with her. From each sacrifice she took what she needed and used the six hybrids, plus Amber, creating veils between the realms and the curtains to Provence City. She then gave Amber back to her family and warned if anyone ever harmed her, or any of the spelled hybrids or their descendants, the realms would be doomed to collapse.

Halsey was very proud and animated as she told the story, and Terra thought maybe she wasn't so bad. In light of that, she gave her a job only the Diama of Navarin could accomplish. She thought it would keep her out of her hair as she figured out how to bring Tania home. Halsey was more than pleased to take on the task.

She stopped at Gwond's after class. It wasn't only Merla's story, but what the ancient text said about hybrids that got her thinking maybe the vampires wanted Tania because she was a hybrid. Was she special in some way? She cringed as the next thought rolled off her brain. Did they plan on turning her? They were running out of time and needed a plan. Instincts dictated that Gwond, being the magic instructor, may have some answers.

He was in his office, alone, when she entered. She knocked lightly on the door causing him to raise his eyes from the stack of papers on his desk, peering at her through his thick glasses. His tail plumage holding a pen, he was using for grading.

"It is only day 3." His tail dropping the pen he was using onto the wooden desk.

She wondered if trolls had specially designed clothes to accommodate their tails. Completely off-topic. She refocused her mind and smiled. "I know and Meesha's been great. She's easy to work with and is helping reach the part of me that communicates with magic, but I have other questions that I don't think she can answer. Not so much about my magic but other things," she rambled, a bit nervous but mostly unsure how to frame what she wanted to say.

Clyde leaped from her shoulder and pattered around Gwond's office. He didn't give the ferret much notice as he focused on her.

His tail pointed toward a chair by his desk. "Take a seat. I imagine you have many questions. It takes initiative to feel you can ask."

His words gave her some comfort and relayed understanding. All this was still very new to her. She took a seat in the wooden chair. It wasn't built for comfort, but she didn't plan on staying long. He was an instructor, so she wasn't sure how much she could say and didn't want to mention anything about Drakonia, Tania, her visits to other realms, or being portalled.

She carefully filtered, which was unusual for her. "When I open up I see, feel, and hear various things that seem unrelated. I can reach the predator magic, such as increased hearing and even vision. I can reach the elfin side and communicate at least one-way with plants. There's another part of me that sees a map of sorts and I feel as though I should be able to manipulate the matter around me."

She thought of how Tania transformed the Aradian rock. She manipulated matter, but not in the way Terra felt she could. In the portal, matter seemed like jelly that she could shape and mold. "I just can't quite do it."

He stared at her, his eyes extra-large behind the thick lenses of his glasses. "Hybrids have skills that are unknown. The tribunal sends them to Lols where they lose any ability to manipulate magic. Their abilities aren't studied. It could be you can manipulate matter. Try this." He rolled the pen he'd been using to grade across the desk toward her. "Move it with your mind."

"What?" She had no idea how to do such a thing. "I don't know how."

He tilted his head and gave her a curious eye. "You have to try first before you decide you can't."

Terra focused on the pen, sending her energy feelers out, but so little radiated from it she couldn't decipher it from the other objects on the table. "How do I find it?"

"Everything has a source. Find its source."

That was vague, she thought. So vague she was glad Meesha was tutoring her and not him. She squeezed her eyes to shut out the visible noise and reached her hand over the pen. She imagined it moving upwards into her hand. It never reached her hand and she popped her eyes open, discouraged at first until she noted it was gone and Gwond had a proud smirk on his face.

As if reading her mind. She wasn't convinced people in Provence didn't do that. She glanced at his tail as it moved around his body, the plumage pointing toward a bookshelf a few feet from the desk.

The pen hung on the edge. "I did that?"

"You did."

She couldn't help but swell with pride and surprise. Another thought came to her mind, unrelated to her conquest, but related to magic. She had an idea, but no one had come out and told her specifics. "What are the levels of magic?"

He raised a bushy eyebrow. "That is a great question. Most often we talk about it, taking for granted you, as a commoner, wouldn't know. Level 3 magic is the hard stuff; portalling, shifting, mind bending and wiping, turning others into stone statues, breathing fire or ice. Level 2 is the softer stuff;

communicating with plants, some telepathy limited to sending a message to someone. Traipsing around someone's mind or visiting and manipulating dreams is level 3. Level 2 are less invasive and don't cause harm. Level 1 is where you are, learning and developing simple magic. Things such as heightened vision or senses."

What she understood was on target. As a proficient reader she comprehended context clues well and was sure he was nudging her to ask. "Is there magic more powerful than level 3?"

He lifted a pudgy, short finger in front of his face. "There is such as the magic that created the veils between the realms, Provence, and the curtains. This is powerful magic that can't be accessed alone or by any living organism in any realm without huge sacrifice." His expression inquisitive but not grim. She was sure hers was.

Merla accessed that magic, and their fear of hybrids suddenly began to make sense. "That's why they fear hybrids. They assume it's possible for them to access level 4 magic on their own?"

He nodded. "Yes, and there is reason to believe that, but that's where you come in." He rested his pointy, short finger on the tip of his nose. "As a commoner you are a hybrid and can demonstrate there isn't a need to fear them. Even if you find you can access level 4 magic, you mustn't use it except to help others. In time, more hybrids will be accepted."

That put a huge burden on her shoulders. She had to be the one to lead the way for equality for other hybrids, such as Cat, who kept her elf side in check and developed her fae side. It wasn't right that she couldn't visit Aradia or demonstrate her unique abilities. "I understand."

"It is a lot for someone your age. You must rely on others for support. Level 4 magic was wiped from history and the books when all this was created so there would be no means to undo or recreate anything stronger or more fantastic."

She thought of the smudged words in the ancient text and wondered if it was redacted, not smudged. There was one more question she had before she left. It bothered her since level 3 magic wasn't allowed in Lols. How did the vampires portal her and Hyacinth back to Provence? "Can someone portal into Provence?"

"Yes. Strong, ancient vampires can portal in, but their abilities are limited. They can't portal anything unless it's something that belongs, and they can't portal out. Level 3 magic isn't only forbidden but blocked." His words more profound than earlier when she'd asked about level 4 magic. Portalling wasn't nearly as grim, but he was a strange one.

In the Shadows

There was a hidden clue in his tone. It was like everything he said had hidden meanings.

She stood then, deciding there was one more important point she needed to make and maybe he could give her some guidance. "This place, Provence, it's like a snow globe. They trap us in here. Everyone else can go home to their realm but me. There's no curtain into Lols."

His bushy eyebrows bunched together. "There's a curtain in Provence, but the only people that know its location are on the tribunal. They don't want commoners traveling in and out at their will, nor do they want us traveling to Lols. What do you know about the realms?"

Her trust radar pointed between confide and almost. "Not much, just what others tell me. Is it possible a hybrid can visit other realms?"

He eyed her suspiciously. "You should be able to enter any realm you are part of. When you enter and exit the first time, you'll get a passport to come and go."

A passport, where she came from, was an identifying document that got stamped when entering other countries. Nalysse had mentioned them in what she assumed was a shade of jealousy. However, she wasn't at 'confide' yet. "Passport?"

He pointed to his chest. "A mark right here."

She could tell she'd asked too much. He might expect answers from her and she wasn't ready to unburden everything to an adult. Clyde climbing her leg was the perfect exit excuse. She swore they had a psychic connection. "I think he's getting restless."

He said the most curious thing as she picked up Clyde: "The answer to your problem is in the tribunal covenants."

Did he read her mind? Level 3 magic was forbidden and blocked. Maybe her questions were just that obvious.

She ran to the portable. The group trickled in one by one and took their places at the table. No one had made much progress. There wasn't any talk around Provence from the few harvesters or any vampires. The ancient texts revealed no more than what they already knew. Nor did anyone have an awesome plan cooked up. In other circumstances, she'd be discouraged, but Gwond's last words gave her hope.

"I stopped by Gwond's today. I figured he could help answer questions about hybrids, and he did. Somehow, I think it's connected to Tania. I understand now why they are feared and how my being here is helpful to all hybrids, or commoners, and he gave me something else." She spat the words out then collected her thoughts. "As I was leaving, he said the answer is in the covenants."

Kinzo responded, "Typical Gwond. His words are always a riddle. It would take too long for us to each read them. I say we divvy them up."

Kayln asked in an airy, effervescent, and sincere tone, "Where do we find them?"

All eyes focused on her and in unsion except Terra, who had no more clue than Kayln, responded, "Our comicays. All the covenants are programmed into them."

Kayln offered a meek smile. This was one question she was happy Kayln asked and mouthed her a *Thank you.*

They divided and conquered as Kinzo suggested, each reading a section. Terra's section was all about using level 3 magic on someone against their will, not in Provence but in the realm itself. It mentioned nothing of Lols or commoners. Not even in the intro of the document did it mention commoners, hybrids, or Lols. The covenants were meant for each of the seven realms.

"There's nothing about hybrids except they get banned to Lols, becoming commoners or being destroyed if they ever return to their realm. There are no laws pertaining to commoners!" Nalysse offered, running her fingers through her hair in frustration.

Caspen's face lit up. "That's it! Commoners have no representation at the tribunal, no covenants protecting them, nor hybrids either. There's not a single thing mentioned about Lols other than banning. Commoners and hybrids are one and the same. Since the covenants don't apply, we have a loophole and can challenge the Tribunal."

26

Tania

If the cuffs and door magically unlocking weren't enough, a male voice in her head guided her safely past the vampires and through a backdoor and underground passageway. Torches lit and expired as she passed them, illuminating her path. Caves were her thing, and she felt no fear of what she might find. Her worries rested with the vampires coming after her once they noted she wasn't there.

The walls of the tunnel were soft. She imagined they'd been carved by blood flow over a long period of time. There wasn't much to see, nor were there any passages into other tunnels, just a long, winding pathway forward. Unsure where it would come out or how deep into Drakonia she was. Was it possible the passage would take her into another realm? Anything in the magical realms seemed possible, but in what other realm might she end up?

She imagined how angry the female vampire would be when she found her gone, and chuckled. Would they send an army of vampires after her? She picked up her pace, her shoes splashing in the trickle of blood beneath them. The cave smelled of rotting body, making it difficult to breathe, but it was her only way out.

The reason Caspen attended the Academy was to learn the covenants and become a diplomat. Challenging the tribunal was not a difficult process. It was democratic and very much underutilized. That was one of the reasons he desired a career as a diplomat. Their job was to find solutions to grievances and too much in the present age grievances went undiscussed. Realm leaders were finding their own solutions, and each realm was drawing more into itself. He believed that was the reason the veils were weakening. How could a tribunal properly function if they didn't do their job?

In the Shadows

Of his friends, he was the only one who didn't have a parent on the tribunal except Hyacinth. Where his parents would be proud, their parents would be upset. Tribunal members met once a week at Provence Hall and didn't appreciate being called on more than that. It was their job, and he was proud to be the one to draw up the letter of challenge.

He stayed up all night drafting the letter. At breakfast, they'd read it over. As a democratic process their input was important. Once the document was ready, they each signed. This wasn't a Terra thing. They all took ownership.

The group met on Provence Hall steps in support of Terra, Tania, and the equality of hybrids – Lols' commoners. It was decided Terra would ring the bell summoning all diplomats to the Hall. Unaccustomed to being summoned, it took a moment for all for the diplomats to arrive.

Upset grimaces and hardened glares met Caspen and the group. He wasn't shocked when they were met with annoyed faces and snarls.

"This is uncalled for."

"Why are we here?"

"Get back to school."

Complaints flowed from their mouths and parents looked on their children with frowns. Once all thirty-five were present,

Caspen stood at the top of the steps, his friends surrounding him in support. "We challenge you. We want to plead our case."

A tall, thick, male, white-haired dragon shouted above the others, "Is your lunch not suitable?!"

Was he the lunch lady's husband? Terra wondered. She was put off by his snide remark. She hated the food, but that wasn't the issue. How dare they be so disrespectful? Heat rose to her cheeks, ready to blow from her ears.

Rosette stood with squared shoulders and pinched lips, her bat wings hiding those standing directly behind her. It wasn't the first time, and probably not the last, she would wear that expression on her face. She hadn't expected much support from her.

No one made a move to further the thing along. Mostly angry glares and disappointment in parent faces. Others snider; at least it wasn't their children.

Terra stepped beside Caspen. There were no rules that applied to her and if they wanted the business aired to the public that's what they'd get. "We aren't children. We are seniors. Our grievance is a wrong that is happening under your noses."

In the Shadows

Out of the circle of woods walked people. From the direction of Navarin, she spotted Cat with other fae. From the direction of Sier: dragons; from Verboten: trolls. That's when she realized they were all hybrids. Their secondary features stood out to Terra more than the dominant ones, such as the taller troll with no plumage in his tail, the dragon without a muscled chest, the short lycan, or the elf with small ears. They gave her more strength than her friends alone. In the crowd, she spotted Gwond with a proud smirk on his troll face. They'd done what he was hoping.

A fae with pink hair and a flowing, light blue dress wound through the crowd and up the steps. She unlocked the doors. Terra and her friends moved to the side as the diplomats filed up the steps and into the building, sneering as they did.

The perfectly circular building had a hall that went around the inside meeting room. Terra spotted a door in the hallway and imagined there were other doors if she'd have been able to follow the hallway. Instead, the pink-haired fae ushered them into the meeting room.

Seven flags, like those at the room in the school, were set at the same seven points as in the Academy room and the passports forming on her chest. The same as the map she'd been working on. Painted on the ceiling was a detailed portrait of the realms without veils between them. It might have struck Terra odd, since the realms were partitioned off, but she was too busy watching everyone else.

The pink-haired fae in her cute dress joined them in the middle. "I'll need your challenge letter to bring to the diplomats. I need one for each realm."

Caspen was prepared and handed her the small stack of letters. Each the same letter. He'd informed them over breakfast what to expect. The fae she assumed was the secretary, as he'd mentioned.

She handed the member in the front row of each realm a copy and they retired into rooms behind them. It was as Terra suspected. They each had a caucus room.

"Once they've all read the letter and discussed it, they will return," said the fae with a smile as she took a seat in a chair near the door and Navarin. Did it matter that she sat by her own kind, or was it merely coincidence?

What kind of diplomats got upset when they were asked to do their job? Obviously, they didn't conduct normal business with others in Provence Hall since they had no chairs. Annoyed, Terra tapped her foot.

In the Shadows

After a walk that felt like an eternity, the tunnels opened to the dry, barren wasteland of Drakonia. So much for ending up in a different realm. The odor of death not so stifling, she took a deep breath, filling her lungs.

She was a few miles outside the city. Buildings towered several stories high. One in the center loomed above the rest. The light sparkled against the windows. She'd been in the basement, she guessed, since there wasn't a single window in any room they'd put her in. She had no idea in which building she'd been held captive. Blood River wound through the city, each building on the edge. Boats as small as, and similar to, canoes to much larger Viking-sized ships were tied around various docks.

"There's a boat tethered ahead. Follow the stream. It will take you to Blood Falls—"

Tania whipped around and would have jumped out of her skin except she recognized the voice. It was the one that spoke into her head. Behind her stood a young man, with his dark hair and eyes he looked Italian, maybe. "Who are you?"

He smiled. "That's not important. You must listen. Once you reach Blood Falls, you must pass under it into Thraves."

Tania studied him for several seconds. He was vampire, maybe, but if that was so why was he helping? "Why should I listen to you?"

"You are the only harvester hybrid alive. That's why you slipped through. Those rocks in your pockets gave me your location when they touched. Now you must get to Thraves and find the harvester inside you."

He vanished as soon as the words left his mouth. "No! Come back!" Her calls left unanswered. She blew out a breath and shook her head in frustration. Why so cryptic and what did he mean by she was the only harvester hybrid alive? She took the rocks out of her pocket and squeezed them together, hoping he'd return. When nothing happened she pushed the small boat into the river then jumped in quickly to avoid touching the blood. She dropped onto her knees with a crash. "Great," she mumbled as pain shot through her.

At this point, anything had to be better than vampires finding her, although she wasn't too sure she wanted the harvesters catching up with her either. After all, they meant to harvest her soul, which she very much wanted to keep.

27

The Tribunal

The diplomats returned in their respective groups of five.

Caspen said they'd each have questions and do some arguing, or debating as he called it.

The pink-haired secretary fae stood. "We will begin. Challengers you have the floor."

Terra cleared her throat and used her most professional voice: "I am a commoner, a hybrid, like the young lady abducted by the vampires – Tania." She thought it was important to attach her name, making it more personal.

She continued: "There clearly are no covenants protecting us nor delegating us to any specific type of behavior conducted inside or outside Lols. Banishment and death do not apply since she wasn't born in Lols, therefore immediate action must be taken to return the young lady home where she belongs."

She twisted as she spoke to get an idea of their reactions, pausing when she reached the vampires. All sat with indignant interest, except one. His dark hair slicked over his oval head, with a smirk on his face. The harvesters each squirmed in their seats. Their eyes a wonder as colors swirled around the iris. Even from where she stood, she noted it. Her eyes were colorful, as if someone splashed paint together and partially mixed them with a brush.

Rosette stood. The harsh expression carved into her face from earlier morphed into one Terra didn't recognize. "Like all of you, I was surprised at the challenge my niece and your children," her eyes rotating to each diplomat parent, "brought forth. I'm proud of her, of them. This is a challenge worthy of our attention. They are right, there are no covenants protecting commoners nor their behavior in any realm, including Lols. Not a single one. The girl must be returned."

Pride, that's what she was looking at in Rosette's face. Terra looked fondly at her, a woman she hadn't liked, but the softness in her eyes and kindness in her words, she was almost proud to be her "niece". Maybe it was the unusual warm fuzzies she was feeling from Rosette, but it seemed there was something else hiding in her words.

A lycan just south of seven feet stood from the front seat, his chest thick with muscle unconstrained by his button-up shirt. His eyes staring right over the tops of their heads and fixing on the vampires and harvesters. "Which of you knew?" When there was no response, he fisted the wooden railing to his side. "Who?! You must answer for your crimes."

This was becoming an inquisition aimed at guilty parties, not Terra and her friends. She'd expected questions, even run through various scenarios in her mind, but not one question aimed at them.

"Lols is a prison and prisoners have no rights. They were banished, end of story." A vampire, not the arrogant one with the slicked hair, but another. His suit and tie made of fine cloth and fit as if custom made.

Another dragon, not the white-haired one who spoke earlier, but a red-haired one like Terra's father, stood. His words as enflamed as his hair: "That girl was never banished. We can't punish children for the sins of their ancestors."

His words resonated with the thirty-five diplomats, as if a meaning was hidden in his words.

A troll from the back stood. "You must answer for this!" he said, with more force than she expected.

The vampire with slick hair and a snide smile stood. "I knew, but only after a harvester came to me for help."

Terra clenched her fists to temper the anger rising inside her. How could he be so arrogant? She wanted to burn the smile right off his face. He was passing the buck. Throwing the harvesters under the bus when they hadn't kidnapped Tania. That was on the vampires.

A harvester stood from the back row. He tugged at the thick, chestnut-colored goatee that hung past his neck. "She fell through the weak veil as a fledgling was attempting his first harvest alone. It should have been easy, but she fell through, landing in Drakonia. I went to Bane. I was wrong in not bringing this to the tribunal first. She evaded us and, once the vampires acquired her, she wasn't returned."

Terra respected that he owned up to his mistake. The guilty parties revealed, she wondered what their future would be.

"How did you find her?" asked a female land fae, noted by her blonde hair and short pointed ears. Her blue eyes focused on Terra.

She swallowed. *This was it!* "I accidently went into Drakonia. I was listening to music, not paying attention, when suddenly I bumped into an invisible wall. When I touched it, it opened." That was the truth, mostly the truth. She didn't think adding that Kinzo was there would further the discussion. It might also get him into trouble with his parents. How was she to know at that point she couldn't go into other realms or even what they were? It was only her second night.

Whispers erupted around the room. It was to her surprise that a female vampire defended her. "It is possible for commoners, not probable, but they are hybrids as were vampires before our second life."

Relief washed over Terra. She was beginning to think being haughty was a trait for vampire delegates. She wouldn't be forced into showing them her passports into other realms or questioned about it. The vampire offered a sound, plausible explanation and did so with a smile. Maybe she was just trying to gain some extra points for team vampire, who'd screwed up royally.

The large lycan from the front row stood. "We must summon Minister M'ra. It is her realm and she is responsible for returning the commoner."

A male fae from the front row spoke after standing, "We will vote."

The diplomats stood and sat, up and down like poppers in Canida. Terra stifled a chuckle at the thought.

The secretary rose from her chair. "All in favor, raise your hand." She did a hand count. "Lower your hands. All opposed?"

That's how they vote? Not very professional. Many more raised their hands in favor, that much was obvious.

The pink-haired fae spoke again. "Drop your paper votes into the box for the official count."

That was more like it. She was sure raising hands for a vote wasn't something done officially anywhere. After several minutes, each dropped a paper into a wooden box near their section. The secretary walked from one to the next collecting then sat at her chair and counted. "Twenty-seven in favor and eight opposing."

Caspen explained there were thirty-five diplomats, five from each realm, so it was an odd number and there would always be a majority vote, unless someone abstained but he wasn't sure they had that choice.

28

Tania

Rowing the little canoe-like boat that wasn't meant for more than two was hard work as Tania was moving against the current. She didn't know what to call the young man who led her out of the tunnels and directed her to the boat. The falls in the distance were still far away.

What did he mean by rubbing the rocks together? It puzzled her, but so did most everything else. She drifted the boat to the shore and rested for a minute, her arms heavy from the chore of rowing. She shook them out and rested as she stared mindlessly at the rocks.

REALM WALKER

Her eyes drifted downward at the sandy shore; something reflected off the sand, drawing her attention. It reminded her of graphite. She picked it up. Its surface was smooth and even though it appeared as though it would split easily in sheets it didn't. She stuffed it in her pocket with the other rocks and with a sigh took the oars and pushed the boat back into the river.

The eternal red sky drove her nuts. There was no sun, only a blanket of crimson. She wouldn't have known evening was approaching if it hadn't been for the portion of moon displayed in the sky.

They hadn't been allowed to leave Provence Hall until the challenge was settled. The diplomats went to their caucus rooms, but Terra and her friends had to stay in the middle room. The pink-haired fae secretary with the cute blue sundress stayed in the room as well, but she had a chair at least. They parked themselves on the floor.

I think it's time for lesson three and the harvesters, Terra thought, depressing the squishy jelly middle of the comicay, directing her thoughts to Meesha.

Sure, like I said, the harvesters are different. They are neither predator nor prey. They take souls and send them into the Otherworld or Tranquility. The veil between the realms and Thraves is thin and their eyes, a vortex of moving colors, allows them to see the dead. When they harvest a soul they don't enter Lols or any other realm in their physical form but as a spirit. That's the only way they can move through the veil. If a soul is dark, they bottle it and send it to the Otherworld. If it is bright and white, they bottle it and send it to Tranquility. In their physical and spirit forms they can enter the Otherworld but never can they enter Tranquility. She sent the thoughts into Terra's mind.

Creepy! What about the blood? she asked.

They drain the blood from all souls which makes up Blood Falls, draining into Blood River. As the blood enters various realms, it is changed. Through the blood, they make life through death possible and complete the circle. Their weakness and their strength is the ability to see and interact with spirits. In a physical form, souls and spirits of the dead can't harm them, but in their spirit form other spirits can harm them, making their job dangerous.

How then did Tania slip through the veil? It didn't seem possible as she was in a physical form. The veil may be thin but how thin was too thin? She stared at the painted ceiling. Unicorns, dragons, wolves, large cats in all realms. Elves tending to all varieties of flora, trolls bent over rivers and streams with pans and tools. Was it that way at one time or was the mural painted in a way that welcomed peace between the realms?

Her thoughts redirected as the diplomats entered into the circular room and took their seats. *Finally!* Terra thought as she and the others stood. The wide doors opened, Devan entered, taking his place with them in the middle of the floor.

The large, red-haired fire dragon that spoke earlier asked, "Where is M'ra?" His tone clearly irritated.

Devan spoke, "She is the minister of Drakonia and a very busy woman. Managing a realm is no easy task. She will channel through me."

Grumbles erupted from all the diplomats except the vampires. The one named Bane continued to wear his smirk. Terra didn't like him. Nor did she understand why the Minister couldn't take a few minutes out of her day to appear. Were most vampires that aloof, or was she concerned about breaking tribunal covenants and the final death?

A female troll with dark purple tail plumage stood and practically yelled, "She's too busy for tribunal business. The circumstances of this are exactly the reason the tribunal was formed!" Her voice firmer than she'd heard from any troll yet.

Devan stayed calm and spoke, "I am Devan Bixler, eldest child of Kevin Bixler, Drakonia's former two term diplomat of the Provence tribunal. M'ra has sent me to represent her." He cleared his throat. "The vampires were acting under my orders. The girl hasn't been harmed." Terra figured maybe this was his punishment. Hyacinth winked at her as if to say *I told you.*

The white-headed dragon who spoke previously demanded: "Your vampires and the harvesters kept from us a commoner in Provence. If we had known, we would have worked together to find her and remedy the situation. Instead, it was kept silent and, to make matters worse, you found the girl and held her in Drakonia. What have you to say?"

"She was in my realm," Devan said in a firm voice.

"Covenant law demands commoners stay in Lols. They have no part in the seven realms. She must be brought to us immediately," said one of the fae diplomats. The eldest. During the break, Caspen explained how the eldest was in the front seat and the more junior diplomats in the back row.

Devan responded with his sexy Australian accent, but the words foreign. "If you can find her, you can have her. We have reason to believe she is heading toward Thraves."

The council erupted, then silenced as Devan spoke as himself. "She's gone and I must return to Drakonia."

Thraves. Why would she be going to Thraves and the harvesters? They meant to take her soul. Would they finish their own mistake? It wasn't like Tania died. She was very much alive. Harvesting her would kill her. Terra's nerves gurgled like a hot spring.

At least the vampires hadn't killed her or turned her…

Tania took a deep breath as she approached the falls. There was no way around. They were layered, one fall dropping into another. She had to go under. Dread didn't even begin to cover how she felt. The blood of dead humans wasn't her idea of fun. She almost wished she was still in the plum room in Drakonia.

One area had a longer drop and the blood was thinner. She paddled the boat toward it. Closing her eyes and lowering her head, she rowed the boat under what seemed the thinnest part of the falls. The boat sailed right through and into a dry cave where it grounded against the cave rocks. Glancing over her shoulder, blood poured over a rocky ledge splashing into the river. She shuddered, happy that was over and desperate for clean water to wash herself off.

The experience brought flashbacks of dropping into the river, her entire body covered in blood.

She left bloody footprints as she moved further into the cave. Almost instantly she noted the air was crisper and fresher. Finally, she could breathe without almost gagging. What did he mean *find the harvester inside?*

Where are you? she called inside her head, then whispered it. *Hello?* The voice didn't respond as she moved further into the cave. *Great! Abandon me now.* Its walls darker and more rocky than the tunnel in Drakonia, unlike Sier she saw no crystals. The further she went the darker it grew. She pulled her phone out but it was soaked with blood and ruined. *Great!* She couldn't even use the flashlight.

She paused and listened. An eerie silence pervaded. There was only one direction to move and she could barely see it. Feeling along the wall, she carefully stepped forward. She'd fallen through once ending up in her current predicament, she didn't want to do it again.

The path leads down, follow it. When you enter the cavern there, you will stop. The voice was back.

Where are you? Show yourself.

He was gone again. She clenched her jaw in frustration. Why was she here? Sure, the vamps couldn't get to her, but the harvesters could, giving them the opportunity to finish what they started. One cautious step at a time, she followed the cave passage downhill until a light emanated ahead. At the end of the tunnel. She moved quicker. When she reached the cavern, she paused. Thick stalagmites and stalactites glowed, lighting the entire cavern. It was beautiful, like nothing she'd ever seen.

The walls streaked with various metals that shone with the light from the cave structures. Opposite her was a rounded doorway. The light reflected beneath the doorway but further behind was cast in darkness. *What is this room?*

She pressed a palm against a stalactite. Warm energy buzzed through her. Pressing her other palm to another, the energy fizzled and popped.

"Welcome," said a female voice.

Tania dropped her hands and turned on her heel in fright. An older woman sat on the cave floor with her legs crossed. Straight, dark hair streaked with chunks of white flowed over her shoulders. She didn't appear menacing and the same warm energy she'd felt in the glowing stalactites flowed from her. She let out the breath she was subconsciously holding in. "Who are you?"

The elderly woman smiled, deep wrinkles carved into her cheeks and below her eyes. "Please sit. I go by many names, but the one you will most recognize is 'Death'."

She lowered herself to the floor across from the woman and sat cross-legged. In her mind, she knew she should be fearful, but the warm energy felt good and familiar.

Death raised her arms to eye level. "The energy of Thraves moves through your soul. You have a special gift and a heavy burden."

29

Terra

After mumbles and confusion from the diplomats, questioning how she was able to enter Thraves, it was decided a search team would be sent to Thraves to find Tania and return her to Provence City. They finally decided there must be a rip in the veil between the realms.

The tribunal challenge over, Terra paced back and forth inside the portable with its drab interior, her nerves tied in a knot. She felt closer to Tania there, remembering their times together as they shared secrets only hybrids could. Nervously, she traced the passports on her chest. Could she go to Thraves?

Every part of her wanted to find out and be the one to bring Tania back, but letting everyone know she could enter so many realms could be dangerous. She wasn't even sure what it meant. Rosette practically begged her to stay at the house, but Terra insisted she needed to be alone. She promised to let Terra know when Tania was found.

Time ticked slower than normal as each grueling minute passed, until Rosette's voice popped into her head. She still hadn't gotten used to it. *They found her and are returning her now.*

Terra nearly dropped to the floor from relief. Collecting Clyde and snapping his harness on, she left the portable.

By the time Terra arrived at Provence Hall, she spotted Tania with a harvester on each side as they exited the woods. It wasn't only Terra who gathered, but all of Provence from the looks of the crowd - even some hybrids who stood in solidarity for Tania's return.

Kinzo, Nalysse, and Kayln sat on the steps of Provence Hall, located squarely in the center of Provence. Without a word, she stuffed the handle of Clyde's leash in Kinzo's hand and ran towards Tania. Collecting her in her arms, she didn't care that she was covered in dried blood. Tania hugged her in return.

She felt good in her arms. "I was so worried about you."

The tribunal agreed to let Tania stay the night, after Terra pleaded with them and her aunt agreed to let her stay with them. Rosette was odd, but no odder than anyone she'd met since coming to Provence, and didn't get why Terra disliked her so much.

When the harvesters came through the doorway, she'd frozen and Death had vanished. The conversation they had, she knew the harvesters weren't going to finish the job. She'd fallen through for a reason and had a job to do. Not one she was overly excited about, but she did understand its weight and why she had to be the one. Death's words moved through her soul. She couldn't run from what she was.

The hot shower was amazing. It was the best shower she'd ever had and she lingered under the water longer than she needed as it massaged her sore shoulders. Terra loaned her more clothes.

She didn't find her aunt's cooking as bad as Terra described it either. For dinner, they had seeds seasoned with something that tasted like a combination of coriander and basil. A vegetable that looked like, and had the texture of, a potato but tasted more like asparagus, and some kind of sweet flat bread. She'd worked up such an appetite rowing, she'd eat nearly anything. Terra, on the other hand, picked at her food until she decided to roll some of the potato thing and seasoned seeds into the bread.

The tension at the table was far worse than the food. Rosette seemed to know something more than she let on. Maybe it was Tania's suspicion. Since falling through the cave, getting kidnapped, and told she had a destiny by Death, maybe she was oversensing things and Rosette was always strung rubberband tight.

After dinner, they retired to Terra's room. She hadn't yet had the opportunity to tell Terra the story, everything, including Death's words and her fate. As they sat on the floor in Terra's room, she told her the entire story. How she was uncuffed and the door unlocked mysteriously in Drakonia, the escape, the voice in her head, the tunnel, the guy who appeared and disappeared, rowing for what felt like forever, how she met Death. If that was the entire adventure and she could go home to a normal life tomorrow, everything would be fantastic. Unfortunately, there was more, and she needed Terra's help.

She pulled out the rocks, including a tip from a glowing stalagmite she collected in Thraves and laid them on Terra's floor between them. "I need two more; one from Verboten and one from Canida."

Terra's eyes widened, her mind distracted by the light emanating from the chunk of stalagmite. "It's beautiful, this one from Thraves. I haven't been there." She picked it up and held it in her palm. "The energy has a pulse, like a heartbeat."

Tania hadn't noted that. She didn't sense energy the same way as Terra. When she touched it, it sent a wave of warmth flooding her. According to Death, she needed rocks from each of her ancestors' realms. She channeled through the rocks. "I don't need specific rocks, any rocks from the realms will work, but we have to go tonight before they send me home."

"Why do you need the rocks?" asked Terra as she laid the glowing rock down and picked up the graphite-type rock.

This was the part Tania wasn't happy with, and wasn't sure how to explain. "I... Um... I'm mostly harvester, but all the realms are part of me and I have a troll connection to the rocks because I have a lot of troll. I have to... do something... other harvesters can't because... I can harvest in my physical form because I'm a hybrid."

Terra's eyes opened wide and her mouth twisted. "I don't know if that's awesome or horrible. You have to leave here, go home and take souls."

"Not exactly. The souls are ones that escaped harvesting. Their ghosts and the rocks will allow me to trap them. That's how Death explained it."

Terra nodded, unshaken by the daunting task. "OK. We can divide and conquer. Verboten and Canida are across from one another. It shouldn't be too difficult. The hardest part—"

Tania cut her off, "No, I have to go to each because I need the mark. Death called it a passport. The rocks won't trap the souls without connecting to the passport."

She could almost see the wheels in Terra's mind spinning. "So you're a lot troll and harvester and only a little of the other things. You can't open Canida's curtain. We'll start there. It's furthest away from here and by the Academy. Once you've collected that rock, we'll go to Verboten. It's beside Drakonia on the other side from Thraves."

Tania leaned forward and wrapped an arm around Terra. "Thank you," she whispered.

"I would do anything to help you." She pulled an arm around her.

30

Once Rosette went to bed, Terra and Tania snuck downstairs, slid the patio door open and slipped outside. There were harvesters positioned outside Rosette's home, but only in the front. After Tania was "lost" twice they meant to keep an eye on her.

Terra felt a slight pang of guilt as Rosette took responsibility for Tania so she could stay one last night. Their mission was more important, and there was no way Terra wasn't helping Tania. If Death gave her a great mission, or destiny, then it had to be fulfilled. She was just glad that Tania was going home; even if it meant harvesting lost souls, at least she wasn't becoming one.

They stayed low and close to the backside of the homes, using them for shadow cover. When they reached the end of the street, they ran into the woods. Wearing all black and dark colors, they blended into the night. Clyde hid inside her backpack.

Since Verboten was close, Tania suggested they go there first instead of the other way around. Terra used her elfin touch to talk with the trees, asking them to distract anyone else that might come into the woods.

When they reached the curtain, Terra easily spotted the etched gemstone in the center of it. She let Tania drop the curtain, almost feeling the sharp pain she would have in the next few hours when four passports were carved into her chest. It felt like carvings, but they looked more like black ink tattoos. For Terra it would only be one, but for Tania it would be Thraves, Verboten, Canida, and Drakonia since she entered and exited from Provence.

Stars shone bright, allowing them to see the thick, grassy landscape, trees and bushes of Verboten. It looked a lot like Aradia, but without all the fluorescent glowing stuff, and ribbons of color danced in the sky, stars shone through, twinkling like magic. Water flowed somewhere near them and they followed the sound. Tania said the rocks would be there.

The journey took them through the woods as they wove through trees and boulder-sized gemstones. Light from the stars reflected on them, lighting their path. The air was fresh and crisp and the energy slow and steady. The idea that she, too, entered Verboten meant she was at least part troll. It didn't surprise her. It would have shocked her if she hadn't been able to enter.

Large nuggets of metal and gemstones dotted the stream which was wide enough to be a river. Blood River; it flowed through all the realms, starting in Thraves with the falls. This water ran clear. The moon and stars so bright she spotted tiny fish swimming around the rocks, as if attracted to the reflected light they gave off.

Clyde stared over the edge of the river but dared not go in. His head bobbed up and down as he watched something moving under the surface.

Tania pulled her pant legs up and took off her shoes to reach into the river for a rock. As she lifted a leg to step into the water, someone approached from the other side. Tania dropped her foot on the shore.

A troll, no more than maybe thirteen, stood on the opposite shore. His pant legs ripped off below the knee. He was the first person they'd met in any realm. Not the first

they'd seen, as they stayed hidden in Sier.
"The stones at the wide part of the river are
too large. The ones downstream are smaller, if
that's what you're looking for," he said,
jumping from one nugget to the next as he
crossed the river. He stopped at the one
closest their side of the shore. "I'm Kyper.
You're the hybrids."

Now they were famous.

"Yeah, we are. I guess that explains
why we're here," Tania said.

He smiled. "That one challenged the
tribunal." He pointed at Terra. "Hybrids from
all realms met in support." He laughed. "I bet
the tribunal didn't know there were so many."

That was the truth. Since it was out in
the open, she wondered if there would be
consequences for them and their families.
Would they be banished? It didn't seem right.
They lived peacefully, hiding part of their
nature. She hadn't even thought about it until
now. She was allowed; they should be too.

Tania glanced at Terra, her eyes filling
with water. "You challenged the government
for me?"

Terra wiped below Tania's eye. "I told
you I'd do anything for you."

Kyper talked about it and how brave
Terra was. She'd become something of an
icon to other hybrids who have stayed in
hiding or were forced to only nurture a single
side of their nature. He stayed on the rocks,

using his tail for balance until the river narrowed and the large nuggets and gemstones vanished. "You can find some good stuff here. A souvenir small enough to take home," he said, jumping onto shore. "You don't even have to go into the water." His tail dropped below the surface of the water, came back up with a shiny metallic stone and handed it to her.

"Thanks. It's beautiful," she said, holding it up and using light from the sky and stars to study it.

His tail dipped again and brought up a couple small gemstones. She studied them too.

"I think I have plenty. Thank you."

He pointed at Clyde. "What is he? Is he a hybrid too?"

Terra smiled. "A ferret. He isn't a hybrid, but there aren't many of his kind left."

He smiled. "He's funny." He paused and glanced over his shoulder. "I have to go home before anyone notices I'm gone. Follow the river and stay on the shore. You got to be careful of the river at night. The thrackers have a nasty sting."

"What's a thracker?" Terra had to ask. She was curious and wanted to know more about each realm. To her, they were all part of her in a way she couldn't explain.

"Fish. They're attracted to the shine of the stones in the water at night."

In the Shadows

Tania stuffed the rocks into her pocket. "Good thing you came along then."

He smiled and waved as he turned on his heel, his tail swinging as he walked. She couldn't tell in the darkness exactly what color it was, but it looked red or maybe orange. Their tail plumage was always bright, warm colors.

They stayed under the cover of the trees as they walked to Canida. Terra worked on developing her predator senses as they moved through the woods. Provence City rolled up its red curtain early, not that there was much to do, which made it easier to sneak around at night under the cover of darkness and trees. She hadn't explored Provence Square yet. There were a few stores, maybe even a couple restaurants. She hadn't paid much attention, and figured so long as they stayed hidden they had nothing to worry about.

She was wrong. Two people standing several yards away, between Aradia and Canida, caught her attention before their voices drained into her ear. She bumped Tania lightly and pointed.

A tall, female teen, Terra guessed a lycan based on her size and toned muscles. "I almost got caught," she complained, her arms around the waist of a guy nearly her height.

His small-pointed ears and shoulder-length lavender hair gave away his fae. "After today, they should be more understanding."

When Terra realized it was two students, she veered to the right. She wasn't concerned, but figured it was better to stay hidden even from a fae and lycan who were obviously involved in a taboo relationship.

Clyde walked between Terra and Tania. The couple, who was now busy kissing, didn't notice as they slipped through the curtain into Canida. The tall grass of the field tickling Terra's legs. She apologized as she picked up Clyde. If there were dangerous fish in Verboten who knows what might be hanging around at night in Canida.

She kept a close eye on the grass and any movements, as well as her ears open, while Tania felt along the ground for rocks. Terra couldn't help the unsettled feeling hackling the hairs on her spine. The energy felt different. It was rougher, as if its effervescence was disturbed.

"I found one. I have to dig a little. It's stuck."

The crack of a stick made Terra whip her head to the left. With her predator senses she spotted yellow eyes glowing through the grass, fifty yards or so from them. "We need to go now."

"Almost got it," Tania responded, unaware of the danger.

The grass moved in a wave directly towards them. "Now Tania." She grabbed her shirt from the back thrusting her upright with a strength she didn't know existed inside her.

"What's all that abou…" her voice dropped off as the wave of grass moved at an alarming speed toward them.

Terra clutched her friend's hand, who seemed to be frozen in place, and pulled her toward the curtain.

"There's two!" Tania shouted as her feet finally started working.

The curtain was only a few feet from them when a large cat lunged for them. All Terra noted was its size and sharp teeth. From the other direction, a massive wolf leaped into the air, catching the cat around the throat and forcing it to the ground.

Blood rushed through their veins like a race car, matched by the quickened thump of their hearts. Neither waited to find out what happened next as they ran through the curtain, stumbling into Provence. This was one situation Terra wasn't curious about. The commotion they made interrupted the couple making out under the stars.

31

"Do you need help?" asked the lycan girl as she rushed toward them.

Terra was still processing what happened. They were alive, and all her body parts were still present and attached. Tania looked to be fine as well, at least she didn't have any notable scratches or worse.

Terra stuttered, "A cat. A really big cat leapt at us."

The lycan lowered her manicured brows. "A cat?" she asked, helping Terra to her feet. The fae helped Tania up.

"It was definitely a cat but a wolf caught it and… I'm not sure," Tania explained, her eyes wide.

Terra hadn't noticed the wolf, but it was Canida. He or she was protecting their realm. Or were they protecting them? Either way, they'd been saved and the cat being bit by a wolf probably wasn't a good scenario, at least if the cat was vampire. Meesha said a lycan bite was a painful death for a vampire.

The girl brought a hand over her mouth. "You sure it was a big cat?"

Terra and Tania nodded in unison. Clyde chittered as if in agreement.

The fae asked the question they were all wondering, except maybe Tania who didn't understand all the predator/prey stuff, "What's a vampire doing in Canida?

Terra shrugged. "A wolf caught it. Should we check?"

The girl shook her head. "You shouldn't. Hybrid or not, can't you defend yourself against a cat that size?"

Heck no! Terra hadn't discovered all her powers, but was pretty sure she couldn't shift into something that large, at least not yet. Would she one day have the ability? At some point in time, she needed to practice magic somewhere outside of Provence where level 3 magic was blocked. "No, that's why we ran."

The lycan went into Canida. Terra wasn't sure it was wise. Lycan or not, she was young and probably not as formidable as an adult vampire, if that's what the cat was. Able to see through the curtain, opened or closed, they watched. Terra was ready to join her if needed. As a fae, her boyfriend wouldn't be any good to her if she was attacked.

That was unfair. Extra realm relationships weren't accepted, but after witnessing so many hybrids today, they'd been happening for some time. In such a relationship one couldn't help the other if assistance was needed within their own realm. Tania was kidnapped by the vamps, but no one could enter but a vampire and they are subject to M'ra, who sounded like a real piece of work. She couldn't even attend the tribunal in person, as if it was too much of an inconvenience.

If the realms were to be separate, why weren't there any who could enter others besides their own? She didn't really understand why, so many thousands of years later, the realms were still separated. In her realm, countries fought, some despised each other, but they weren't separated in a sense that kept them from entering. Some had frivolously built walls and, in the past, a large body of water was a barrier, but there was always a way in.

There was no sign of a cat or a wolf. It was a long, few anxiety-filled minutes before the girl returned. "They're gone. This is really bad. I won't mention you were here, but I have to call my dad. He's a diplomat." She turned to her fae boyfriend. "You need to leave too. If my dad knows about us—"

"I know. You don't need to say more." He pressed his lips to hers in a kiss.

Terra's heartbeat finally returned to its normal resting rate as they neared Rosette's house.

"I was really scared back there," Tania said, putting her hands on Terra's shoulders. "I have to go back. I have a job to do. This place, it's not safe. Not after the past few days and what I saw back there."

Terra ran a finger along Tania's cheek. "I'll be fine. I have friends. I'll be careful."

"Promise?" Tania raised her hand from Terra's shoulder, displaying her pinky.

Terra hooked her pinky around her finger and Tania pulled her closer, their lips meeting in a kiss.

32

Terra's bed was big enough for the both of them as they snuggled around Clyde, his warm breath against their chests. Terra pet his head then pushed it gently toward Tania. She could handle the pain of one passport, but four would be unbearable. As if the ferret understood, he snuggled close to Tania.

Terra could hardly sleep from worry. She watched Tania with a close eye as she slept. As the day broke, the stinging pain burrowed into her chest as the new mark was inked. She took deep breaths, her chest tightening with each until the pain was unbearable and she wanted to scream. Then it vanished.

Terra woke to an empty bed. Even Clyde was gone. She pulled herself up, panicked for a moment that Rosette took Tania home without waking her. Once fully awake, and hearing Tania's voice downstairs, she realized that hadn't happened.

She pulled her shirt up in front of the mirror and inspected. The mark was barely an outline of a gemstone, like the one in their flag.

She made her way downstairs, not hungry when she spotted breakfast on the table. It was the same bran-ish type muffins as Rosette served Terra's first morning in Provence City.

Rosette agreed she could stay home from school to see Tania off. Terra didn't come with much except the clothes she wore when falling through the cave and her cell phone. They left those clothes at the portable. She figured eventually she'd throw them away. Blood stains didn't come out easy.

Rosette left the room to tend to her garden. Terra used that opportunity to ask: "Did you get four more passports?"

"Yeah, they are light but I can see them forming." She pulled her shirt down, or rather Terra's shirt that she was wearing. Below the dragon was a crossed pair of pickaxes, below that an infinity symbol, under that a gemstone and, above Aradia's tree, a wolf's head.

Why did they use the pickaxe? They harvested in spirit form and Tania was to use the stones, so why a pickaxe? Tania didn't have an answer.

She walked with Tania as far as Provence Hall. Rosette wouldn't allow her to go further. "We'll meet again," Terra whispered as she held Tania in a tight hug. Somehow, she knew they would. She felt it in the same way she understood other things.

"When you figure out how to portal." She pulled away, brushing Terra's hair behind her ear. She tickled Clyde under the chin and kissed the top of his head. "Take care of her."

Terra watched as Tania entered the building. The tribunal members all present followed her inside the hall, the secretary closing the doors behind them.

Was the portal in there? If so, it was hidden well. Around the meeting room were seven doors, one for each realm. The hallway went around the meeting room with a door to each realm's room. Where was the portal?

Slowly, she walked towards campus. Her mind speculating where the portal was, she remembered Gwond said there was a curtain. Certainly, if there was a curtain in Provence Hall she'd have noticed, unless it was hidden in a room or… below.

Halsey was in class when she arrived at the room. She hadn't had much sleep the previous night, between keeping an eye on

Tania and dealing with the pain of the passport as it inked into her skin. Her eyelids heavy, she lay down. Later, she'd try her magic. She'd seen at least a partial map of the realm. If she could get there again, maybe she'd find the curtain.

Drifting into lala land, she popped her eyes open when Halsey burst through the door.

"What are you doing? Get up! Get up!" Halsey barked.

Terra wasn't in the mood and forgot all about the "special thing only the Diama of Navarin could do" mission she sent her on. "Later." Terra rolled over in her bed, turning away from the bubbling blonde fae.

"You can sleep later. I promise you, you want to do this now," she said, practically begging.

It was Terra's idea. She let out a deflated breath and dragged her body upright, remembering the special thing. "OK."

When they arrived in the cafeteria, Halsey practically skipped. In a corner was a kiosk of sorts. It was exactly what Terra requested. A counter above a cabinet stocked with disposable plates, silverware, and cups, she noted as Halsey opened the door. A dorm-sized refrigerator was parked next to the cabinet. It had its own freezer! And it was stuffed with food, everything she asked for and more.

Terra had to give it to her. She accomplished exactly what she asked. She'd given her list to the Dean, but that had been days ago, and she'd made no progress. In a couple days, Halsey had everything.

"This too," she said with a satisfied smile. Opening the other side of the cabinet, there was ferret food, not any ferret food but the kind she got from the vet.

Terra gave Halsey a cheeky smile. "You like Clyde."

"He's not so bad."

She threw her arms around the fae princess. "Thank you, from me and Clyde."

Halsey returned the hug. Maybe she wasn't so bad. There was hope for her anyways, and life in the dorm might improve so long as she kept her entitlement shoved into a drawer and locked.

"Show me how you work that thing?" Halsey asked, pointing to the microwave.

With Tania safely home, the tribunal met for a special session. This was customary. The same as all members being present as she was portalled into Lols. They considered it best practice, as the curtain would be a journey from her college campus. Now the business was over, it was time to close the event and retire home.

Lukas, the eldest lycan, stood. His words casting a shadow on everyone present. "Last night, a large cat was seen prowling Canida. A lycan took it down with a bite into the throat. It got away. Our work today isn't done. We must close the veils immediately."

Ernessa, a female vampire, stood. "You tell us a vampire was bitten by a lycan and your only concern is the veil?"

"The vampire was in our realm. It tried to attack Judge's daughter. Yes, it got bit!"

That was a new development. It would be known soon enough who the guilty vampire was. Rosette guessed it was an older vampire, as it was able to shift and get away, which meant it probably portalled. As vampires aged, they gained powers. It's been said M'ra has the ability to shift, portal, and mind bend.

Terra and Tania had snuck out after she'd gone to bed. She wasn't sure how they got past the harvesters, nor did she ask. Terra had a habit of not wearing her comicay, like the day she stumbled into Drakonia. Rosette remembered she'd taken it off to shower. There'd been times she'd attempted to contact her but got no answer.

Inside, she smiled at the crafty girl. She knew the devices tracked movement. The fact that she was exploring realms was good. She needed to explore them all to find her true powers. It wasn't up to Rosette to stop her. It was difficult not to say something as each realm she entered got her closer to who she was. She wanted to explode and tell her everything, but reminded herself – "not yet".

Presently, they had a new situation. She was on the side of mending the veil. If the vampire suffered, it shouldn't have been where it didn't belong and she'd bet it didn't go after Judge's daughter but Terra. There was something about her people liked. It wouldn't be out of the question to think the lycans were covering for her. She even had a lycan teaching her to access her magic.

Olivia, the junior fae, stood. "We have enough potion made to give each realm. Once every realm has theirs the last ingredients of limestone and hemlock will need to be added last as they will trigger the reaction that will seal the veils. They can't be added until you are ready. It is suggested by the fae that all realms be sealed at the same time for maximum strength. We will be doing ours again too."

"We vote now to do that tonight," Maglesh, the outspoken troll, suggested.

The tribunal agreed. The vote was taken, and it was unanimous that it would be done tonight. Each realm would add the final ingredients at the same time. She hoped it did work, as it would give Terra the time needed.

"We aren't finished yet. We have another vote to take," Colton, the fire-dragon, glanced towards Bane then Metford. "We must remove Bane and Metford. They cannot serve on the tribunal any longer."

It wasn't even a discussion and Rosette fully agreed. She needed to worry for Terra's safety, especially since she seldom wore her comicay, making it difficult to watch over her. The best way to keep her out of harm's way was to have diplomats who weren't plotting behind the tribunal's back.

The vote was taken and agreed. New elections in Drakonia and Thraves would choose two qualified diplomats to fill their shoes.

33

Terra waited outside Gwond's door. It was their time to meet and she had more questions. After eating, she'd fallen into a deep sleep, waking early in the morning when the energy around her suddenly changed. It was as if the fabric holding the realms together tightened.

Instinctively, she channeled the magic surrounding her until the map and lines were formed, starting from her and not as rudimentary as in the past. They drew outward, encompassing the school, and that's when she noticed above her was an entrance to another realm.

The lines became clearer as they drew past the school, past Provence, and through the realms, some more detailed than others and in them were fractures of various sizes. The breaks came together as if someone pulled a zipper.

The door opened and the students rolled out of class, taking her from her thoughts.

The troll stood by the bookshelf in nearly the same spot as the day she and Meesha stopped in. "Is it day 5?" he asked.

She nodded.

He leaned against the bookshelf. "You did a good thing this week. Not everything needs magic to be solved."

"I'm getting better at controlling it." He'd given her solid information and was at the trust level. How to say what she saw was another story. The words stumbled as they dropped from her mouth. "Last night… something happened. I'm not sure how to explain it. It was… as if someone… zipped the realms together."

His expression unchanged, as if this wasn't news, he said, "Indeed. You are in touch with the magic." He raised a bushy eyebrow. "How many realms now have you entered?"

What did that have to do with anything? Was he going to give her another puzzle she had to solve? "All but Navarin and Thraves."

REALM WALKER

"Navarin." He nodded his head as his tail moved around his legs. "It may be time for you to visit. Merla was a clever fae and to make sure her spell that created the realms never be undone or tried again she wrote it in a special scroll she called the Realm Grimoire…"

To be continued…

The Land of Lost Souls
REALM WALKER VOL. 2

1

alsey burst into the dorm, her face contorted as if she'd robbed a bank, her blonde hair styled to perfection. She pushed the door closed.

Terra looked up from the book in her lap. "Did you get it?"

"Of course. I'm the Diama of Navarin." She unfurled her palm, revealing a shiny golden key. "This could ruin me. I have expectations to live up to. We need to make this quick. I have to return it before the Dean notices."

When the veils were strengthened with the fae potion, the tightening of the fabric between the realms woke Terra from a solid carbohydrate-induced sleep. At that time, she noticed a curtain – the entrance and exit to a realm – above her. There was only one higher level than the dorms at Provence

Academy. The one with the cupolas that they kept locked.

She informed her friends, and since her roommate, Halsey, came through for her with the kiosk filled with commoner, or human, food she decided she would entrust her with "borrowing" the key to unlock the door to the stairwell.

After all, sometimes it was better to enlist those you didn't truly trust into covert activities. It put them in an awkward position, forcing their silence. Halsey, as the Diama, or princess, of Navarin, had a lot to lose if it was discovered she'd helped. Probably more than anyone else on campus. She was also a fae, same as Dean Salena, which made her Halsey's servant. It was good for Halsey they didn't plan on keeping the key longer than overnight.

Halsey sat with her "ladies" at dinner, as she always did, bossing them into waiting on her while Terra joined her friends in the courtyard. Other than as roommates, no one knew they tolerated one another. Nothing was amiss.

"Will you take Clyde?" Terra asked, practically stuffing the handle to Clyde's harness in Kinzo's hand. The first friend she'd made since coming to Provence City. He was an attractive male specimen of an elf. A day ago, he'd changed his hairstyle a bit and now wore two braids on each side of his head and tied the rest of it in a ponytail that trailed all the way down his back. His tall pointed ears interrupted the flow of the side braids but gave them a sexy touch.

She trusted all her friends with Clyde, her chocolate brown-footed ferret, but he liked Kinzo the best which meant he usually got to be ferret sitter when she grabbed her food. She hadn't brought Clyde back into the cafeteria since the white-haired dragon lunch lady caused so many problems about having an animal in the lunchroom.

She covered a microwave burger in a paper towel and cooked it, then grabbed herself a chilled coffee from the fridge. It was nice having a kiosk to herself and if she'd gone any longer not having commoner food she might have wasted into nothingness. She didn't want to push it yet, but thought a toaster oven would be a nice addition. Microwave fries weren't the same or as crispy as oven baked ones.

Nalysse, Kinzo's elf girlfriend – that's how she always thought of her – tickled Clyde's chin as Terra sat down. He ran his front paws through her long hair. It wasn't that she didn't like her, or was even jealous, it was something else she couldn't really define about Nalysse.

There was a silly elfin belief that their long hair helped them communicate telepathically with plants, and sometimes insects. Terra thought it hooey, especially since she, too, only part elfin, could communicate with plants. Her short, bobbed hair didn't hinder her. It was at this point a one-way conversation, but once she learned to manipulate magic better she hoped it would become two-way. The plant communication class she was taking was a big help. She was curious about the types of things plants thought about. It wasn't like they had a brain; but who knew, maybe the ones in Provence and other nonhuman realms did.

Caspen, also an elf, his hair long but also super curly so it didn't appear long, swallowed a drink of something orange and set it on the table. "Did she get it?"

"Yup! We're on for tonight," Terra responded with a grin.

Meesha held her fist to Terra for a bump. She was a lycan: tall, dark, toned, and beautiful. She was also Terra's magic tutor.

Hyacinth sipped on her chilled blood bag. She always put a straw in the top. "Lights out at 10. Terra, you should go first and unlock it so we can file in one by one instead of all at once. We'd make too much noise, and someone would notice." She was the only vampire in their group, but Terra was the only hybrid. Hyacinth was also Caspen's girlfriend. Extrarealm relations were frowned on, except with vampires, since they were infertile.

In the Shadows

They all accepted each other, including their differences, even Kayln – a water or sea fae, depending on who's telling the story. All fae had a smug attitude. Kayln wasn't an exception, but wasn't smug in the same way as Halsey. She was a bubblehead, and generally not snooty on purpose. Terra figured it was in the fae DNA.

Terra set Clyde out a bowl of food then turned her attention to the group. "She's coming with us," she said, meaning Halsey.

Their faces didn't hide the disappointment. No one actually liked Halsey. "It has to be this way. The further involved she is, the less she will implicate us and the more she will help cover things up." Terra laid it all out.

Not a single one of them knew for sure what secret realm had a curtain on the fourth floor of Provence Academy, but all had a good guess – Lols or the Land of Lost Souls. Or, in the terms Terra thought of it: home.

She'd been in Provence City all of four weeks. In that time, she'd entered five realms, rescued Tania – a human who fell through Thraves as her soul was meant to be harvested. She landed in Blood River in Drakonia – home of the vampires. After rescuing her, she had to get her home, but Tania ended up a prisoner of the vampires, eventually escaping to Thraves and finding out she was part harvester.

Terra and her friends challenged the Tribunal – a once in a lifetime event – and got Tania home safely. The caveat is that, as a harvester-commoner hybrid, she can harvest souls in her physical form. Full harvesters could only do it in their spirit form, which meant Tania now had to seek and save lost souls.

After dinner and chilling with her friends, Terra retired to her dorm to catch up on homework. Halsey was there when she arrived, doing what she loved to do – toss clothes on her bed to find the perfect outfit for the next day.

"I can't believe you are actually going through with this. It's crazy and you could get in real trouble," Halsey said, with a hint of spite.

Halsey wasn't worried about Terra getting into trouble. She was concerned that if Terra did, Halsey's part would be revealed. "So are you."

Halsey dropped the shoes in her hand. They clanked on the wooden floor. "I will not!"

"You will, but leave the comicay here. That's how they track us and spy on our memories." The comicays were sticky, clear gel things that stuck to their arms, a hair above the wrist. They worked similar to cell phones, but were more advanced.

Halsey blew out a frustrated breath. "I got you the key. You don't need me."

Terra leaned against the pillows smashed along the headboard of her bed. "No, but admit you're curious."

"Maybe, a little. The tiniest bit."

Terra didn't need her along to appease her curiosity, but to hide the crime. A Diama was a powerful weapon in her hands. "Yeah, that's why we're going."

Halsey dropped the discussion and, when 10:30 rolled around, she followed Terra into the hall. She left Clyde asleep on her bed. She took him everywhere, but wasn't going to wake him. Their room was only about ten feet from the door that led to the stairwell. Terra slipped the key into the lock on the infinity-handled door and pushed it open.

The entire school was designed to be inclusive of each realm except Lols. The door handles were infinity symbols for Drakonia and vampires, the walls sparkly lavender for Navarin and the fae. The banister was jeweled for Verboten and the trolls, and more. Everything was designed for everyone.

The coast clear, they slipped inside the room. Terra, instead of flipping the light switch which might alert others there was someone on the fourth floor, turned her cell phone flashlight on. It couldn't make a single call from Provence City which lacked cell towers, being in a different realm and all, but it still had uses.

The beam of light displayed the same shimmery lavender walls as the rest of the school. The wooden steps weren't floating like the ones that went to the first, second, and third floors. These were wooden steps smashed between two walls.

Halsey shut the door behind her. A voice in the hallway caught their attention. Halsey's face contorted in agony. Terra motioned for her to stay still. Footfalls moved toward them and the door opened.

2

Halsey let out such a long breath, Terra expected her to deflate like a balloon. Meesha, whose room was across the hall and down a couple doors from Terra and Halsey's, entered. Hyacinth behind her.

The four girls went up the stairs, Terra in the lead. When she stepped onto the fourth floor, she instantly noted a change in the energy. It pulsated like a heartbeat. She stopped after a few steps and spread the light from her phone across the room. It was empty.

Flashes of familiarity crept up her spine. *Had she been there?* Four walls and wooden floors. The walls weren't shimmering lavender like every other wall in the entire school. They were a drab, cream color. She went to the closest window and glanced out. A door creaked below her, followed by footfalls. Terra turned off the flashlight on her phone and froze. The other girls followed.

Capsen's voice split the eerie silence, "Hyacinth, Terra?"

Terra turned her flashlight on and spread it toward Caspen's voice. He and Kinzo stood at the threshold of the stairwell. Caspen, spotting them, stepped across the threshold. A ripple of energy forced its way through Terra, and again as Kinzo stepped across.

She didn't have any idea what that was about. It was curious, but so was what she spotted outside the window as she quickly beamed her flashlight across it. Thick green trees. Trees in Provence weren't all green, some had silver, bluish, or even lavender leaves. She stared at the green foliage and, in the distance, mountain tops. They weren't in Provence anymore.

She assumed the change in energy and ripple she felt was due to them crossing the curtain into Lols. "Take a look," she said, "outside the windows."

Halsey joined her. Her mouth dropping when she saw unfamiliar territory. "We're in Lols." A profound statement for Halsey.

To Terra, it was home, only it wasn't San Francisco or even California. She assumed it was somewhere northeast, in the Blue Ridge and they were somewhere in Tennessee, Kentucky, North Carolina, Virginia, or any of the other states the mountain range sprawled through. The thick, bushy trees that weren't sequoias gave it away and the mountain range was much smaller than the Rockies.

Kinzo glanced around. "Shine the flashlight to the other end. There has to be an exit."

Terra did. The room was empty of any furniture and the other end was dark. Even the light didn't reach it. Terra walked forward, at a slow and steady pace, the light guiding her.

"Shine the light to the left?" Kaylyn asked.

Terra did, illuminating a passage. Nalysse, who was the last to join, said, "Come on." The excitement of the adventure filling her words and movements as she was the first to take a step onto a narrow, winding staircase that reminded Terra of an emergency exit in a hotel.

It seemed never ending until they reached a final landing. A door at the end with a deadbolt. Nalysse paused in front of the door. Glancing behind her for approval from the group, she flipped the dead bolt.

"Wait," Terra called, moving sideways past her friends to join Nalysse. She opened the door and stepped outside, trying the key in the door. "It doesn't fit. Someone will need to stay behind."

Halsey piped in, "I will."

A silent groan moved through the group. No one trusted Halsey to be the one.

Meesha spoke up, "I'll stay too."

Terra felt the relief, as everyone trusted Meesha. Lycans in general were a trustworthy subspecies. Fae were snooty, self-centered, and generally not trustworthy; add that Halsey had the most to lose. She'd probably go back to the dorm and leave them all there, then concoct a story about Terra sneaking out of the dorm in the middle of the night.

Terra took several deep breaths, allowing the pine scent of the trees to fill her lungs. Trees in Provence gave off a eucalyptus-myrrh scent that smelled good but was annoying when that scent was all she smelled on a daily basis.

The air, wherever they were in Lols, was fresh and crisp and wet. The moisture in the air filling her lungs. As a west coast girl, she was used to dry air. A chilly breeze swept over them. It felt good to Terra. There were no breezes in Provence. She likened the place to being trapped in a snow globe.

Hyacinth joined Terra. "I think we're in Virginia, close to Cahas Knob." Noting the surprised expression on Terra's face, she continued, "I grew up in Boone's Mill, only a few miles from here."

Terra had never asked Hyacinth about her life before she died and became a vampire, partly because the opportunity never arose and partly because she didn't know how difficult it would be for Hyacinth to talk about it. She was sure she still had family in Lols and imagined never seeing them again was painful. Every day since her father's death, she missed him. Even though she'd never known her mom, she missed her too, as she thought of the pink carnation tattoo on her ankle that stood for her mother's undying love.

Hyacinth stared towards the mountain range. "I miss them, but its better they don't know I exist. It would be harder for them to see me after burying me. It was a beautiful funeral." She paused for a moment to collect her thoughts. "I was nine and got sick. I was born with a weak immune system. A cough snowballed into pneumonia. My body couldn't fight it off." Her voice, even though sad, was filled with positive energy.

Terra didn't really know what to say, but she was rarely speechless. "I miss my dad. I'll never have the option of seeing him again hanging over my head. How do you do it?"

"I've seen them, but they didn't see me. Devan's portalled me a few times. I'm good with watching them sleep or eat dinner. My little brother is fourteen. My sister started college two years ago at Virginia Tech. I can live with knowing they are happy. I can't physically join them, but I can share in their happiness and success."

Devan was her adopted vampire brother. Vampires were wildly diverse. They were human before being given a chance at a second life. Hyacinth was a young vampire and certainly hadn't lost her humanity. The vampires that kidnapped Tania she imagined as older, with little to no humanity left. "That's beautiful."

Hyacinth smiled. "This is beautiful." Her eyes still fixed on the sprawling, endless mountain range.

Since Hyacinth was speaking freely about her human life, Terra had a question she'd been curious about. "Do you keep your names when you are reborn?"

A breeze carried a few strands of Hyacinth's hair toward Terra, tickling her cheek. "No. We choose our first name. It can be anything we want and our last name we get from our adoptive parents. I used to be Jenni Pham."

The name she chose fit her better, in Terra's opinion. She had a hard time seeing her as a Jenni. Her dark, straight hair, olive yet pale skin tones, and almond-shaped brown eyes, along with her upbeat personality, made her think of a flower not a Jenni.

Kinzo wrapped an arm each around Terra and Hyacinth's shoulders. "That view is gorgeous. Reminds me of Aradia, but with highlands. Turn around, though, and look at the view behind you."

The school. Behind them was the school. It didn't strike them odd at first until they realized they weren't looking at the school. They were in Lols, not Provence.

Down to the very last detail, the brick structure was a complete duplicate of Provence Academy looming above them. But only the structure. The grass, Terra noted, was overgrown and shared space with knee-high weeds. The trees hadn't been trimmed in years, if ever, and ivy grew up the side of the building. "It's a duplicate. The school can't be in two realms."

"No, it can't, but we aren't alone either," Hyacinth said, then took off at phenomenal speed, vanishing into the woods.

"Hyacinth!" Caspen called, then took off after her.

She was much quicker as a vampire. Elves didn't have supernatural speed. Terra couldn't let him go alone and shot off after him, stopping abruptly when she spotted Hyacinth's green shorts, and then her blouse. She collected the clothes, tucked them under her arm, and caught up to Caspen who stood frozen.

His eyes fixed forward. The sight sending shivers down her spine.

3

A large, red-striped cat, its paws stretched forward and head low, growled at a much smaller bobcat. *Hyacinth.* Besides incredible strength, speed, and increased senses, vampires could also shift into large cats, mind bend or wipe, or portal. Younger vampires generally had one of the three skills, but older vampires could master others.

Terra and Caspen stepped back. The bobcat was no match for Hyacinth. Before their eyes, the bobcat morphed into a human teenager. He twisted his legs and covered his privates. Terra glanced away, as he'd lost his clothes the same as Hyacinth.

The rest of the group caught up and stood beside a shocked Caspen and Terra.

"Where are your clothes?" Kinzo shouted.

The wild-eyed teenager glanced at him then Hyacinth, and nodded his head toward the woods. Terra tossed Hyacinth's clothes toward her. They landed beside her front paws.

She collected them between her teeth, glanced at Terra as if to say thank you, and sauntered behind the trees.

"Hold hands," Nalysse requested, one of her hands on a tree trunk.

The comment directed at those who were elfin, as they could communicate with trees. Holding hands, Nalysse on one end and Terra on the other with a hand pressed against the same tree trunk, all thought: *Please bring him his clothes.*

The tree stretched its branches upward, as if waking from a long slumber, followed by the tree next to it, then the next. It triggered a chain reaction. The teen's clothes were dropped from a low branch onto his dark, wavy-haired head.

They decided magic, not just low-level magic but level 3 magic, was present in Lols and dormant, which isn't what they learned in school. This conclusion made sense since Hyacinth and the teen were able to shift. That took level 3 magic. The instructors insisted Lols had no magic and when one went to Lols they lost their magic and memories. They'd proven both wrong. No one had forgotten anything, and magic definitely existed. If it hadn't, neither Hyacinth nor the teen would have been able to shift and the elves couldn't have "woken" the trees.

The teen's name was Mario. He hadn't been spying on them, and couldn't explain what happened to him. It started happening in recent months and he didn't understand it or have anyone to talk to about it. He didn't live far away, and ran to the school when he changed because it was empty.

"The sun will be up soon, and my father will get up for work. If I'm not home, he'll notice," Mario explained. His brown eyes no longer bewildered, but pleased. He thanked them before going on his way.

Hyacinth sighed. "He's right. The sun will be rising soon." Deflated, she turned back toward the door they exited. "It's gone!" she exclaimed, running to where the door had been.

The door had vanished. Terra and the others joined her, feeling along the wall.

"Mario said this place is abandoned, why don't we just try the front door?" Caspen suggested, calmly.

Hyacinth wrapped her arms around him. "I'd burn without you!" She kissed him on the lips.

Technically, if the building was a true replica of Provence Academy, they should be able to enter through the front, go up to the third floor and enter the stairwell leading to the fourth floor, therefore entering Provence. But they came down a spiral stairwell, exiting out the back.

"The door is locked," Nalysse said as she pulled the knob.

In the Shadows

Kayln flipped her lavender hair back and blew on her finger. The sun peeking a smidge over the horizon. She drew a circle around the lock, then poked the middle and said, "Druppo." The door slid open.

Terra assumed the word meant unlock, or something similar, in fae. Hyacinth bolted inside as the sun continued its rise over the mountain tops. Caspen quickly closed the door while they slid the curtains shut to keep out the sunlight.

Terra confronted Kayln. "If fae can unlock doors, why did we need the key?"

A smug smile crossed Kayln's face. "Because our sigils use fairy dust. It lasts at the site for about six hours and can be spotted by any fae. Dean Salena is a fae. I also think Halsey wanted to be involved, after all, she could have opened that door herself."

Terra didn't disagree. In fact, she was pleased Kayln was siding with her in her attempts to involve Halsey. She wondered if she could enlist them both with her plans in Navarin. Merla was a sea fae. According to her limited research, it was Merla who used strong fae magic to build the veils between the realms. Kayln was a sea fae and Halsey was the fae equivalent of a princess.

Her gut said she needed to start in Navarin's Lavender Seas if she wanted to find Merla's Realm Grimoire. It never occurred to her she couldn't cross Navarin's curtain, even though that made no sense since one could only enter the realms in which they had ancestry.

Halsey didn't offer, or even mention, fae could unlock doors. She wanted to be involved. Well, Terra had something else Halsey could help her with. She was sure being the diama had its perks, but it didn't make her a cool kid. Rebelling and not getting caught did.

Terra walked alongside Kayln. "The word you said, what did it mean?"

"Open. Our spells use the old fae language. We learn it from a young age, but only use it in spells."

Every day she learned something new about these supernatural realms she'd only just learned existed.

The building, structurally, was identical, but the walls were drab white not sparkly lavender. No cerulean, eternal teardrop flowers vined the floating staircase from floors one to three. The gemstones and bronze weren't embedded in the banister. The doors outside didn't sport the pickax handles and inside were regular knobs instead of infinity symbols. The septagonal room under the stairs was present but absent the flags from the seven realms. The dragon-lycan fountain in front of the school didn't exist.

The large, thick curtains in the entryway were creamy and tattered, but they blocked the light. Years of dust covered the entire empty building. On the third floor, they went left as they would to get to the female dorms. The boys were to the right.

Terra appreciated they didn't discriminate based on gender. That didn't save them from discriminating against hybrids, although they hadn't made a fuss and forced massed banishing of all the hybrids who came forward to support her when she challenged the tribunal.

Caspen closed the open doors as they reached the third floor, keeping the sunlight off Hyacinth. Terra admired the care he took to be sure she was safe and could cross without turning into a ball of flames.

A wave of relief, followed by anxiety, passed through the group as Kayln unlocked the door to the stairs the same as she did the front door. No one knew if the stairs would be present and lead them back to Provence. In theory it should, since the building was a replica. Crossing her fingers, Terra entered the stairwell behind Nalysse.